"Did you just arrive in Norcastle?" she asked pointedly. He could tell she was fishing.

"I came in on the bus last night."

"Were people shooting at you before you came to town?"

"Nope. Is this how you welcome newcomers?"

"Hardly. I'd lose my job for sure. I will find out who did this, Mr. Stone."

"Oh, that's easy. I already know who wants me dead." He grunted as he slipped his arms in a chambray shirt, stained with dirt from many hours on the job.

"Well, do tell. I can't help you if you're withholding information."

"The Spencers."

Sylvie let out a laugh. Such a loud, robust sound for a little lady. Ian pictured the chief of police issuing orders in the same tone. People would take notice of her, although she'd had his attention long before she opened her mouth to speak.

Katy Lee writes suspenseful romances that thrill and inspire. She believes every story should stir and satisfy the reader—from the edge of their seat. A native New Englander, Katy loves to knit warm, woolly things. She enjoys traveling the side roads and exploring the locals' hideaways. A homeschooling mom of three competitive swimmers, Katy often writes from the stands while cheering them on. Visit Katy at katyleebooks.com.

Books by Katy Lee

Love Inspired Suspense

Roads to Danger

Silent Night Pursuit
Blindsided
High Speed Holiday

Warning Signs
Grave Danger
Sunken Treasure
Permanent Vacancy

HIGH SPEED HOLIDAY

KATY LEE

HARLEQUIN® LOVE INSPIRED® SUSPENSE

Recycling programs for this product may not exist in your area.

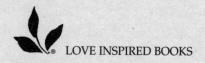 LOVE INSPIRED BOOKS

ISBN-13: 978-0-373-44779-4

High Speed Holiday

Copyright © 2016 by Katherine Lee

www.Harlequin.com

Printed in U.S.A.

You intended to harm me, but God intended it for good to accomplish what is now being done, the saving of many lives.
—Genesis 50:20

To my dad, John. I love that you are my biggest fan.
And I love you.

Acknowledgments

I am so grateful for my editors
at Harlequin Love Inspired Suspense for their help and
insights in making the Roads to Danger series come alive.
Thank you, Emily Rodmell, Shana Asaro and Giselle Regus.
Your enthusiasm made all the difference.

ONE

Was a cop ever really off duty?

Chief of Police Sylvie Laurent didn't think so. She freed her hands from her wool gloves and pocketed them in her winter police coat.

Then she unclipped her gun holster.

Trouble never waited for her to clock in, and it wasn't about to start now.

Even when it posed as a good-looking man sporting a golden tan.

"You're not in Kansas anymore," she mumbled aloud, heading the stranger's way. Or, with his bronze skin maybe she should say Cali.

He appeared like a black sheep against a sea of snow white—the snow-covered grounds of Spencer Speedway, as well as the paled complexions of the townspeople he pushed through. It would be months before any of them glowed a golden bronze like that, maybe not ever.

So, who was he? And why was he here?

A group of local children with cotton candy frozen to their cold faces cut in front of her, innocent to the possible threat at the annual Jingle Bell Jam celebration. The Christmas event put on by the Spencer family for longer than Sylvie could remember wasn't a tourist attraction. It was something the Spencers offered to their employees every year to start off the holiday festivities. That included pretty much everyone in Norcastle, New Hampshire, but it did *not* include this guy.

A horn from the racetrack blew. Sylvie kept walking, even though she knew she was expected down in the pits. The small 1940s reproduction cars called Legends were set to compete on the track in ten minutes. Sets of snow tires strapped under the carriages of the tiny vehicles would give the crowd some excitement as the teen division of drivers raced to the finish line in the annual Legends snow race. Her son would be among them—and expect her to be on the sidelines.

Duty calls. Sorry, Jaxon.

The stranger's eyes met hers, chilling her with their hold. There was something about their ice-blue color that was so familiar. With one blink, he took them away and dismissed her.

Bad move, mister.

Sylvie picked up her steps to cut him off, but three teenage boys stepped in front of the guy, blocking her path. Just a few feet from making contact, she ran into one of the boys, knocking something to the ground. A glance down and her plans changed in an instant.

A can of beer lay in the snow.

She picked it up. "Belong to you?" she asked one of the teens, noticing his bulkier-than-normal parka. A closer look at all three boys, the same age as her fourteen-year-old son, and she noticed they were all smugglers today.

Sylvie took her last look at the black sheep's retreating back and decided he would have to wait.

"Unless you boys want to be cuffed and stuffed in

the backseat of my cruiser, I suggest you hand over the alcohol you have in your pockets."

Bret Dolan, the son of Norcastle's mayor, flicked his straight, dirty blond bangs from his eyes and lifted a defiant chin to Sylvie.

Like father, like son.

"I don't know what you're talking about," the boy spouted. "That's not ours. That was already on the ground. We just have a couple sodas." The boy lifted a cola out of his pocket. "See?"

Sylvie reached inside her navy blue uniform coat. "Shall I call your parents, Bret, for the show when I search you? I'm game for an audience." Sylvie took out her cell phone. She checked the bars and saw none, but she didn't let on about the lack of coverage, which was spotty in these mountains on most days.

On a huff, the Dolan kid reached into his other pocket and withdrew a can of beer. He jammed it over to Sylvie.

"Crack it open and pour it out," she instructed without touching it.

"Really? You can't be serious." Bret's distaste for the whole event became even more evident as each of the boys followed suit with the same task, their lifted spirits at getting away with something doused right along with the six-pack of beer now on the snow around them.

"I'm very serious. I care for your safety, Bret, even if you don't see that right now."

"You don't care for me. You just hate alcohol because your mother drank herself to death when you got knocked up."

The horn from the racetrack blew again, but its penetrating sound paled in comparison to the pulsing of blood pumping behind Sylvie's ears at Bret's remark.

She bit back a lethal response. She was sure the boy was only repeating what he'd heard his father say. "Why aren't you racing today, Bret? You should be out there."

"Mind your business," the boy spouted off. Again his dad's words. She let Bret's disrespect go...for now.

"The next time I catch you, I take you in," Sylvie said. She looked Bret in the eyes, holding his attention on her. "Tell your mom I said hi."

He blinked a few times. Then he sent her a scathing look as his friends dragged him away.

She hoped someday he would see that she cared for his safety, his and his mom's. She prayed it would be soon. For now, though, she had a stranger to find.

Sylvie hit the button to her radio on her shoulder. "Preston, Buzz, Chief here. I know you're at the track. Be on the lookout for an adult male in his early thirties, shaggy black hair and black leather coat, about six feet in height. Not from around here. Just want to make sure he's not about to cause any problems."

"10-4, Chief" came a response from one of her lieutenants.

Scanning the crowds in the grandstand and still finding no sign of the black sheep, she entered through the fence marked Authorized Personnel and sought out the number eleven coupe her son drove. He weaved his tiny yellow car in a wavy line with the other racers, who were warming up their reflexes for the start of the race. The yellow flags waved, but as soon as the lead car approached the starting line, it would be go time.

She hadn't missed it after all.

As a single parent with a full-time job there was a lot she missed in her son's life. It caused a wedge.

She sighed at the growing distance between her and her son and thanked God that Jaxon was behind the wheel today and not smuggling alcohol with Bret and his gang.

Thank You, Lord, for watching out for him when I can't. Just as You watched out for me fourteen years ago. You never left me to raise him alone.

Unlike Jaxon's birth father.

Unlike everyone else in her family.

The starting horn blared. The green flags waved like crazy. The crowds behind her in the towering grandstand cheered. The race was on.

Sylvie watched her son take the lead from the number eight car. His tiny vehicle roared as its motorcycle engine was pushed to the max. She fisted a hand in the air. "Go, Jaxon!"

Her son had been racing cars since he was six, starting with little go-karts. It wasn't a cheap sport, by any means, but Sylvie worked extra shifts to give him something he could be proud of and work toward, something that kept him off the streets. She hadn't been too excited about him following in his birth father's footsteps, but she lived in a racing town and it was hard to steer Jaxon in other directions. Her brother was out in the world following circuit after circuit, racing on tracks in strange and exotic locales now. She'd barely heard from him since Mom had died.

Jaxon lost the lead, and Sylvie snapped out of her reverie, especially when his wheels swerved off to the left.

What was he doing? Sylvie rushed forward a few steps, but knew she couldn't get any closer to the track to find out. She scanned the area for Roni Spencer Rhodes, her son's trainer and owner of the racetrack. Would Roni know if something was wrong?

Sylvie spotted her friend in a white down coat and matching hat and scarf, her long red hair whipped a bit in the cold wind. She wore a headset that had to be connected to Jaxon. Sylvie headed Roni's way, but as she approached, she noticed out of the corner of her eye someone else approaching Roni.

The stranger!

He had no business being behind the fence.

His ice-blue eyes targeting Roni dead-on said otherwise.

The race became immediately forgotten. Sylvie reached for her weapon. "Stop right there!" She raised her voice to be heard over the motors.

The unidentified man came to an abrupt halt.

Sylvie took three determined steps, her hand curled around her gun's handle. A bang from the track echoed through the valley, bouncing off the surrounding White Mountains and back again.

The man flew forward at her and fell to his knees. Sylvie withdrew her gun and took aim. The crowds in the grandstand inhaled and shouted at the same time. Had they all seen her draw her weapon?

Or was something else going down on the track that claimed their attention?

A quick glance showed a mass of cars piling up and flipping. Number eleven's wheels were overturned.

Jaxon!

Sylvie wanted to run to him but the stranger now lay facedown on the snow, blood spatter around him, stark in its rich contrast of dark on light, like the man himself.

He was injured.

But how?

Torn between him and her son, Sylvie holstered her weapon and dropped to the stranger's side. A hole in the arm of his leather coat showed where an object had entered his body. Something flying off the track?

She inspected at a closer range.

No. A bullet.

Sylvie took in the perimeter in short, jerky perusals for a shooter in the area.

No time. She had to first take care of the victim.

She lifted the man under his arms and dragged him behind a snow pile. A groan told her he was conscious.

"Sir, I'm Chief Sylvie Laurent. Can you tell me your name?" she yelled over the ensuing chaos around her.

"Ian Stone," the man groaned and moved to turn.

"Stay still, Mr. Stone. I'm calling for help." Sylvie reached for her radio.

"No!" The man raised his good hand. "No help." He pushed himself to his knees. Blood seeped from his left shoulder, his other hand stretched across his wide chest to staunch the flow.

"Ian, I need to get you to the hospital. And you need to stay down. The shooter is still out there."

He shook away from her grasp. "Help the drivers. Not me." He stood up and mumbled, "I should have known they would take me out. I should have known this was too good to be true." He half ran, half staggered to the fence exit. The alarmed crowd of spectators behind it swallowed him whole.

A war waged in Sylvie. She had to go after him. What if he bled out and died? She couldn't have a murder in Norcastle. And a murder it would be. She knew a gunshot when she saw one. The crash had muffled the sound, and the mountains…

Sylvie looked to the lofty peaks overlooking the racetrack.

The mountains were hiding a killer. The marksman could be out there somewhere on Mount Randolph. He could go after Ian Stone again.

Sylvie hit her radio to call her team, but all emergency personnel were flooding the track to help the drivers, the kids.

The place she needed to be, too.

Jaxon.

Sylvie zeroed in on her son being lifted from his car, awake but limping, his pale blond hair that matched her own shielded his eyes, but he was talking. Her heart lodged in her throat as she watched him enter one of the ambulances opened and ready to whisk him off to the hospital. The police and paramedics had everything under control, and he was in good hands.

Sylvie stepped in the direction Ian Stone had staggered off in, the direction she was needed most.

Her conflicted steps turned to a full, determined run.

She'd known Ian Stone was trouble the second she'd laid eyes on him.

But apparently, someone else did, too.

Ian slammed the door of the studio apartment he'd rented the day before. Carrying a pharmacy bag, he put it between his teeth as he tore off his coat and dropped it to the wood floor of the old factory mill, now turned into living quarters. The brick building was one of many along the river in this old New England mill town—a place he supposedly had been born in thirty years ago, but hadn't known existed until two weeks ago.

The bullet hole in his arm said someone wasn't happy about him finding out.

Pain from his shoulder seared like an unrelenting burn. Of course it had to be his already injured arm. Two weeks ago he'd had surgery on his shoulder for a bad rotator cuff, an injury he'd had for years but left unrepaired for lack of funds. Working construction these past two years for Alex Sarno had finally given him enough to check himself into a hospital for the procedure.

But how would he pay for a gunshot wound?

The Spencer money perhaps? And not because he'd taken a bullet on their property. According to the guy who'd shown up in his hospital room after the surgery, their money was also his money.

All these years he had an inheritance to claim and never knew.

Thirty years ago, a car was pushed over the side of a mountain. The crash left two very rich parents dead and their three children orphans. Except when the smoke cleared and the blaze was extinguished, only two children were accounted for. Little eighteen-month-old Luke Spencer's body had never been recovered.

Instead, he grew up across the country in a cabin in the Washington mountains, playing the unwanted son to Phil and Cecilia Stone.

Ian bit hard as he ripped off his green T-shirt, the words Sarno Construction scrawled across the front. His wound seeped blood, but not at an alarming rate. He would live to collect his inheritance and soon the T-shirts would read Sarno and Stone. Alex had already offered him a partnership. The idea of being a business owner was more than a dream come true. Things like this didn't happen to Ian Stone, or Ian the Idiot as his father called him too many times to count.

But he wasn't Ian Stone, if he believed the guy in his hospital room. He was the missing sibling, Luke Spencer.

Judging by the poor welcome home, however, his brother and sister didn't want to share the wealth. But would they take another shot at him to see they didn't have to?

Ian bounded around the sofa bed and pulled the blinds closed just in case. With his teeth he ripped the package of cleansing wipes open.

A bang on his door jerked him alert.

"Now's not a good time!" he shouted. He hoped it was just the landlady, Mrs. Wilson or Wilton, or whatever. A busybody was what she was. So many questions. *Where are you from, Mr. Stone? Do you have family in Norcastle, Mr. Stone? Perhaps I know them. What are their names?*

"But at least she didn't shoot me," he muttered, then seethed when the alcohol splashed over his wound.

The door knocked again, harder.

"Go away!" he yelled, biting through the pain.

"Ian Stone, this is Police Chief Sylvie Laurent. I need you to open this door."

The cop from the track? The one with the eyes. Great. "I did nothing wrong. Leave me alone!"

"Sir, I didn't say you did anything wrong. But you were shot right in front of me. It's my job to make sure you live. Open this door, or I will call for backup and do this the hard way."

Backup? That's all he needed, people in uniform taking sides. They'd probably arrest him for extortion. Ian figured he could play the victim to the little slip of a woman they called chief. The fact that she was the chief stumped him.

She shouldn't be too hard to get rid of.

Ian opened the door ajar. "I'm fine, Officer, really. I can take care—"

The door banged in on him with a force that sent him backward. She jammed a thumb over her shoulder as she pushed past him. Dark blotches of blood drops lay stark against the snow behind her. "You're dripping. You are not fine. Now take a seat," she commanded, pointing to the stool at the breakfast bar.

The cop washed her hands, ignoring the fact that Ian remained standing. She removed a pair of latex gloves from a compartment on her belt. "Sit," she said and slapped them on.

He obeyed and she quickly cleaned his wound and prodded around for the bullet.

Her ministrations killed, but Ian wasn't about to let on in the presence of this small, but tough, woman. While on the stool, their eye levels matched.

Green.

He smiled.

"I'm sorry I'm hurting you," she said without glancing up from his wound.

"Hurting? Nah, not at all. I could stay here all day." He leaned closer to her face, zeroing in on her almond-shaped eyes. "They've got to be jade."

"What does?" she asked absently.

"Your eyes. They're the inspiration of epic poems. Marlowe, Yeats, Ovid. I'm not sure any of the greats would do them justice. When I saw you at the track, I thought it was a trick of the sun, but it wasn't. Has anyone ever told you how beautiful they are?"

A startled look from under long curved lashes came his way. Her eyes narrowed. "Has anyone ever told you, you are a glutton for pain?" She pushed her finger through his wound.

Ian yelled out and bit down under her digging. He moaned and gagged and stopped breathing as she continued, succumbing under her thumb to being a puddle of feebleness.

Her gloved fingers removed the bullet and she held it up to him with a brilliant smile of victory. "Got it."

The slug blurred in front of him and he gagged again. "I think I'm going to pass out." He'd still yet to breathe.

"It's possible. You also need stitches to stop the bleeding." She put the bullet in a small plastic bag she took from another belt compartment and reached for the bandages. "I need to take you to the hospital."

"No." Ian straightened, swallowing the bile rising in his throat. "You obviously know what you're doing. Just do what you have to do and stitch me up."

She applied butterfly bandages to pull the holes closed, but shook her head. "Sir, these won't hold. You need to let me take you."

"You gonna pay for it?"

She stilled her hand. "You don't want help because of finances?"

"More like lack of them."

"You don't need to worry about that."

"You obviously never had to enter a hospital without a way to pay for your visit."

The chief frowned.

He'd upset her. The idea of hurting her made him feel like a creep. "I'm sorry. I shouldn't have said that."

"We all have our stories, but I can tell you the hospital will not turn you away, no matter what yours is. Trust me. Let me bring you. It's only about a thirty-minute ride."

"Thanks, but you can save the gas."

"I have to go there anyway. That crash at the track? My son was in it. He's probably already flipping out that I'm not there."

Ian studied the officer's face for what she wasn't saying. He detected a glimpse of fear, and suddenly she wasn't just a cop. She was a mom. "Was he badly hurt?" Ian asked.

Her eyelids closed on a sigh. "No, I thank the Lord that he walked away. Barely, but he walked." She reopened them and got back to work on his arm. "So you see, I do need to get over there. We're all each of us has."

"No dad in the picture?" He felt odd asking, as if it was any of his business.

"Not needed." Her answer was even stranger.

But then Ian thought of his own old man, and understood her statement perfectly. "The man who raised me died recently. I hadn't seen him in ten years. Not needed. I get it."

"So, you'll let me take you?"

"I have a feeling that's not really a question."

"It's not, and every second that goes by is making my son feel abandoned."

"Way to tack on the guilt. Fine. For your son's sake. Let me grab another shirt, then my coat…what's left of it."

Sylvie taped the gauze in place and he reached for his duffel bag, his clothes still jammed inside, unpacked.

"Did you just arrive in Norcastle?" she asked pointedly, obviously fishing.

"I came in on the bus yesterday."

"Were people shooting at you before you came to town?"

"Nope. Is this how your town welcomes newcomers?"

"Hardly. I'd lose my job for sure. Any idea who did this?"

"Yup." He grunted as he slipped his arms into a chambray shirt, stained with dirt from many hours on the job.

"Well, do tell. I can't help you if you're withholding information."

"The Spencers."

Sylvie let out a laugh. Such a loud, robust sound for one so small. Ian pictured the chief of police issuing orders in the same tone. People would take notice of her, although she'd had his attention long before she opened her mouth to speak. Still, he didn't like her laughing at him, and that's what her reaction felt like.

"What's so funny, Chief?"

"You are. Roni and her brother Wade are not trying to kill you. You're completely wrong about that. Why would you think they want you dead?"

He snatched his MP3 player and headphones from the bag and stuffed them in his front blue jeans pocket. "Because they have something that belongs to me, and they don't want to give it up."

"Well, I don't believe they'd put a bullet in your arm, no matter what they have of yours, but I do plan to find who did pull the trigger. There hasn't been a premeditated murder in Norcastle in thirty years, and I want to keep it that way." She opened the door and scanned the area before telling Ian to follow her to her cruiser.

"Who was the unfortunate victim, then?" Ian asked—as if he didn't know.

Sylvie opened the passenger-side door for him, then came around the front of the car. Once behind the wheel, she replied, "Actually, it was Bobby and Meredith Spencer. Wade and Roni's parents."

And mine.

Ian faced front, revealing nothing to the local PD. He couldn't be sure the police could be trusted. After all, his parents were murdered, pushed over the side of that mountain in their car, and the police thirty years ago called the crash an accident.

Had the police been a part of the crime?

Did they know why he had been taken from the scene?

Ian peered out from the corner of his eye at Sylvie. It was too soon to tell her.

He looked to her eyes again. Long lashes curled like a perfect Pacific Ocean wave. He didn't believe them to be fake. She wasn't wearing a swipe of makeup. Perfect, creamy skin, a hint of blush from the cold. She looked like a porcelain doll, so pale compared to his baked skin.

"You hanging in there, Stone?" she asked, giving her attention to him for a brief moment while she drove. "You look a little…off. Not feeling light-headed, are you?"

"Just a bit," he said, but had to wonder if it was more from her presence than the loss of blood. He cleared his throat and scanned the mountains out his window. "I'm just not feeling the love in this town."

"You'll be safe with me, Ian. I promise I won't let another shot find its mark. It'll be me before it will be you."

TWO

The emergency room buzzed with standing room only. Sylvie bypassed it and led Ian up to the front counter. "Good evening, Liz. I've got a GSW in the arm. Any way you can get him in? He's bandaged well and the bullet is out, but he still needs stitches."

"Anything for you, Chief." The front-desk nurse pushed a clipboard over to Sylvie.

"Can you also tell me where Jaxon is?"

"Curtain three."

"Great, you'll find us waiting in there. Stay close and follow," she said to Ian.

They passed by the waiting room and a familiar red-head jumped up from her chair and rushed their way. "Sylvie, hold up!"

"Walk with us, Roni," Sylvie said without halting her steps. Her friend joined them down the hall. "How's Jaxon?"

"He's a champ, but what took you so long getting here?"

"Roni, meet Ian. Ian, Roni Spencer."

"I know who Veronica Spencer is," Ian said, his voice hard and condemning. Did the man still think Roni tried to kill him? She was watching the track when everything went down. She couldn't have shot him.

"Have we met?" Roni replied.

"No, we haven't," Ian clipped.

"But you know me. Are you a fan?"

"Figures you would think so, but no. I don't follow racing."

Sylvie leaned into Ian. "You're barking up the wrong tree, Mr. Stone. Watch it."

"It's all right, Sylvie," Roni assured, but her normally bright smile dulled. However, Sylvie quickly noticed a mischievous glint spark up in the woman's ice-blue eyes. Her friend never got offended, even when the joke was on her. She just angled those ice crystals on the other person and gave it back tenfold. A quick glance Ian's way, and Sylvie noticed his eye color had the same hue. That's where she'd seen it. Wade and Roni had the same eyes. Interesting that Ian's eyes matched the Spencers'. Before Sylvie could speculate further, Roni said, "I'm sure your Ian will smarten up soon enough. It won't take too long for him to realize what the town revolves around."

"I assume we're talking about you again?" Ian shot back.

"Ian!" Sylvie nearly grabbed his injured arm and threw him behind a curtain—any curtain would do. "She was talking about racing. Now knock it off. Roni is not your enemy. And, Roni—" Sylvie leveled her eyes on her friend "—he is not *my* Ian."

Roni pursed her lips. "Good, because you could do so much better. He reminds me of all the locusts claiming to be our long-lost baby brother lately. We got another one this week. Now that word is getting out that Luke didn't die in the car crash, strange men are coming out of the woodwork. Don't they know we will have them tested?"

"Right," Ian said with a smirk, "because you can't let a penny of your money go to a locust."

"All right, that's it." Sylvie made a grab for Ian's good arm and twisted it up his back. He didn't fight her as she pushed him toward curtain three. "Get in there before I throw you out the front door and let whoever shot you have another go at it." That part she whispered, but not softly enough because her son immediately spoke from behind the curtain.

"Shot?" Jaxon said.

Sylvie opened the curtain to shush him. Anxiety she'd held at bay since the accident lifted from her shoulders at the healthy sight of him. She shoved Ian inside and turned back to Roni to see if she'd heard, but her friend only said, "He's cute, and a worthy opponent, but watch yourself." Sylvie wanted to set the record straight. She was in no way interested in Ian Stone. In anyone for that matter. But she knew her friend would never stop hoping she would find someone someday, like Roni had found her handsome FBI agent, Ethan Rhodes.

Sylvie yanked the curtain closed with a rattle to the metal rings above. "Sit in that chair and fill this out." She passed over the clipboard and went to her son's bedside to hug him, relieved he let her embrace him. After a few moments of assurance that he was alive and well she pulled back and picked up his chart to read. "How you feeling? Anything broken? Has the doctor seen you yet?"

"Leg snapped. I'm getting a boot. Who is he?" Jaxon asked, peering around Sylvie.

"He's someone I brought in for stitches."

"Because he got shot?"

"Yes, but's that's between us. Don't go repeating that. I'm keeping him with me until I know more details." Sylvie turned to see Ian hadn't even clicked the pen to write his name. "The doctor won't be able to see you until that's filled out, Mr. Stone."

Ian barely looked at the forms. "I told you I didn't need this. I shouldn't have come here."

"Just why *did* you come to Norcastle? Especially if you don't follow racing."

"Is it a crime to want to see a mountain town in New England at Christmastime?"

"No, but you don't fit the profile of a tourist, most know how to dress appropriately for the harsh winters. It snows practically every night up here. Did you even pack a hat and gloves? A scarf? I'd say you're a California man. Am I right?"

"I'm impressed."

"I don't care if you're impressed." She nodded at the clipboard. "Just write it."

Ian stared at the information sheet and clicked the pen. He clicked it again and again. Five more times at a rapid rate before he sent the clipboard clattering to the floor and jumped to his feet. He was out the curtain in an instant.

But he wasn't faster than Chief Sylvie.

She had an arm wrapped securely around his neck and had him back behind the curtain and in his chair before anyone saw the takedown.

"Man, you thought you were going to escape my mom?" Jaxon said with a wry smile. "I could have told you not to bother. She's got some moves."

Ian cleared his throat and mumbled aloud, "'And though she be but little, she is fierce.'" He ran his fingers through his hair to right it back into its unkempt style. He straightened up in his chair. "How about a warning next time, Chief?"

"It wouldn't change anything. She'd still win." Jaxon smirked.

"Thanks a lot, kid," Ian said, chagrined.

"Was that Shakespeare?" Jaxon asked. "That quote about my mom being little but fierce?"

"Yeah, *Midsummer Night's Dream.*"

"I'll have to read it."

"Here." Ian reached into his pocket and withdrew the MP3 player. "I have the audiobook on here. You can listen to it."

Sylvie picked the clipboard up and held it out to Ian again. "If this is about money, I already told you not to worry. It'll get worked out."

Ian stared at the floor. "It's not about the money. At least not all of it."

"Then explain. What was that outburst for?"

He hesitated, but then blurted out, "I can't read, okay?" His gaze lifted to her.

"Whoa," Jaxon said, but Sylvie warned her son with a shake of her head before he could say more.

"You should have just said so," she said to Ian.

"I try to avoid being ridiculed whenever possible." He looked away. "I have dyslexia. Words and letters make no sense to me. They're all one big wavy line, moving around the page."

"We won't ridicule, right, Jaxon?" Sylvie said.

"No, man. I get enough of that at school to know it stinks." Jaxon reached for the clipboard. "I can help you fill it out."

Sylvie's heart swelled with pride to see her son jump in to help a complete stranger with no judgment. But she did wonder what her son meant by experiencing enough ridicule at school. He hadn't mentioned anything to her before about it. And it couldn't be for his academics. The boy excelled in every subject.

Sylvie's cell beeped with one of her lieutenants calling her. "Excuse me for a second," she told the boys, but they didn't seem to notice she'd said anything. The two were laughing about something Ian said was a ridiculous question on the sheet. She walked behind the curtain. "Preston, I'm glad you're calling. I have a non-resident who's been shot today. I need to get a report going."

"A GSW? Drug related?"

Sylvie glanced at the closed curtain. "Possibly. The victim hasn't given me much to go on, other than blaming it on the Spencers. I'm thinking he's hard up for money, maybe owes someone. They retaliated by pulling the trigger. Anyway, I have the bullet. I'm bringing it in. I'll need you to run ballistics."

"Got it."

"So, you called me. What do you need?"

"Nothing so full of grandeur. Just that I think I'm right about Smitty and Reggie. I found a business card for an ecologist specializing in salt contamination in Smitty's desk. You know I think Officer Smith has been instigating the picketers over at the salt shed. He wants Reggie back as chief." A recent wave of protesters had sprouted up in town, vocalizing their disapproval about the state of the shed that stored the season's road salt.

"Reggie is retired from the force and doesn't want to come back. Trust me. I'll talk to the people over at the shed. I realize they're worried about contamination of the river, but this is going to have to wait until I get home. Maybe even after Christmas. My son is injured."

"Is Jaxon all right? I heard that he was going to be okay."

"He is. But his leg is broken."

"Should I come down?"

"Thanks, Preston, that's nice of you to offer, but I need you holding down the fort.

I should be back in Norcastle in a few hours."

"What about Smitty and Reggie?"

"Like I said, Reggie is retired and Smitty will be up for retirement this year. I'm not worried that they want my job. They've been on the force for over thirty years, and I think I have shown them they can pass the baton. My probation period will be up in two months, and the town council will approve my position as permanent. I need you to stop worrying and just follow my orders."

Preston huffed. "Right. Hold down the fort. It's all you think I'm good for. I know others who would disagree."

The line went dead. Great, another ego she would have to console.

After Christmas.

Sylvie turned on her heel and plowed right into Ian's wide, very hard chest. The guy did some manual labor for sure.

"Is everything all right?" he asked. His piercing gaze saw too much…and sent a tingle up her spine.

The effect baffled her.

"Yeah, of course. Why wouldn't it be?" Her voice squeaked.

Her voice *never* squeaked.

She gave orders like a drill sergeant. Deep, loud, so there was no mistaking the fact that she was in charge. She snatched the clipboard from his hand.

Ian Stone
Construction worker for Sarno Construction
Pasadena, CA.

"Pasadena, huh? I thought money was an issue for you."

"It's temporary. I live in a trailer on the construction site my boss is working on. We're building a development. Homes that I will never sleep one night in. I just build them and move on."

She eyed him over the clipboard. Maybe Ian Stone was moving on to other ventures. Like setting up shop in Norcastle to sell drugs.

If that was the case, he would quickly learn he'd picked the wrong town to target.

And the wrong cop to dupe.

"I don't need a shadow," Ian stated against Sylvie's plan for security detail. He pulled on his coat slowly. "I just need a ride back to my apartment."

She glanced her son's way. "The doctor wants you to stay the night. Do you mind if I leave for a while to bring Ian to the station? I want to keep an eye on him to make sure no other bullets find their way into him. You okay with me leaving, Jax?"

"No, but since when does that matter?"

"Jaxon, we made a pact. Remember? I accepted the chief position, but only because we understood the sacrifices would be on both of us. A team."

Jaxon shrugged. "Yeah, I know what we said. It's just…"

"Just what?"

Jaxon avoided his mother's questioning gaze. "Never

mind. It's nothing. Just go. I'm tired anyway. I'm just going to go to sleep."

Sylvie hesitated at her son's brush-off. Ian thought her frown expressed a bit of sadness about something going on between the two of them. But she quickly snapped back to her stoic self and patted Jaxon's good leg. Whatever it was wouldn't be hashed out tonight. "Okay, kiddo, they're getting a room ready for you. I'll be back as soon as I can."

Sylvie turned to Ian. "Stay by me." She took the lead and Ian gave a single wave to her son.

"Bye, Ian."

"Take care of my player, kid. It's my window to the world."

At the exit they stepped out into the freezing night. Sylvie held an arm up to survey the parking lot. "Looks clear."

Ian stifled a laugh at the absurdity of the situation. *She* was protecting *him*?

If nothing else, Ian had to think Sylvie took her job seriously. He had to figure his previous concern to trust her had been unwarranted.

Still his lips remained sealed.

But so did hers. Something weighed on her mind, if her chewed-up lower lip was any indication.

It wasn't until they made it to the interstate that Sylvie broke the void. "All right, I want to know why you're in town, and I want the truth. Are you here to sell drugs?"

Now he did laugh. "What? Drugs?"

"I want to help you, Ian. Please let me."

He sobered. How many times in his life had he hoped to hear those very words? Hearing them now put him in uncharted waters. What would happen if he accepted the offer?

He decided to trust her and find out.

"No drugs. But I am here for my cut."

"Cut of what? Somebody owe you something?"

The vast blackness of the New Hampshire night shrouded and protected him. His shoulder hurt, but not only from the bullet hole. A memory that predated any surgical procedure to fix the injury caused by an abusive father flowed vivid and clear. No money in the world would ease that pain. "Nobody owes Ian Stone anything. But Luke Spencer has an inheritance coming to him."

Sylvie slammed on the brakes, screeching the car to a halt on the side of the highway. She jammed the car into Park. "Are you telling me you think you're the long-lost missing Spencer sibling, Luke Spencer?"

"Not think. Know."

"You heard Roni. They've had a slew of men staking the claim. They *will* run tests."

"Already done and passed."

Sylvie's dashboard lights illuminated her shocked face to an eerie version of her sweet, good-natured self. "Do you have any idea how much pain Wade and Roni have been through? The possibility of finding their missing brother has been a light at the end of a horrifying tunnel."

"Meaning they'll be highly disappointed they get *me*? That obvious?" He tried to sound indifferent and shrug it off, but deep down it hurt because he knew they would be right. He wasn't Spencer material. He was an illiterate drifter. Not a racing star like his sister or a United States Army captain like his brother. And he couldn't forget the grandfather in the CIA. The family was full of overachievers.

"Well, maybe if you had been a little nicer, they would be more accepting," Sylvie said.

"And maybe if they hadn't tried to take me out, I would be nicer."

"I already told you the Spencers are not trying to k—" Sylvie's words were cut off as headlights from behind neared the cruiser. The car slowed as it came up alongside the driver's side. Sylvie rolled down her window and waved them by.

An unmistakable silhouette appeared out the car's window.

"Gun!" Ian yelled and pulled her down with him as a bullet whizzed through the car and smashed out the passenger-side window. The car sped up and screeched away.

"Are you okay?" Sylvie yelled.

"I'm fine. You?"

"Fine." She jammed her cruiser into Drive. "Hold on. I'm not letting this car out of my sight." She radioed for backup to be ready for the shooter heading into Norcastle.

"You'll never catch him," Ian said as she sped up.

"Thanks for the vote of confidence, but they don't hand out chief of police badges to just anyone. I did have to prove my ability, even if some people don't think I did." She mumbled the last remark.

"I'm sure you're a fine cop, but that is a paid assassin up there. When there are millions of dollars on the line, people will pay out big for an experienced hitman to make a problem go away. Those types of professionals generally don't let themselves get caught."

"So you're back to calling out the Spencers as shooters? They would never be involved in anything so devious."

"Then what about their CIA grandfather? I'm sure he's got at least a handful of assassins on speed dial."

Sylvie did a double take. "How do you know about him? That's top secret information. The Spencers don't tell anyone about their grandfather's job."

"Michael told me himself." The use of their gramps's name silenced her. "Michael Ackerman, some head honcho at the CIA, showed up in my hospital room two weeks ago. I went in for surgery on my shoulder for a torn rotator cuff. I woke up to find him sitting in the chair beside the bed. Apparently, he found me just as lacking as you do. It appears with all this shooting, he's now wishing he'd never found me and is trying to get rid of me. If I were you, I'd think twice about going after one of his hired guns."

"News flash for you. I'm the chief of police. That means I go, no questions asked." Sylvie radioed for her officers to be aware that the perpetrator was a possible assassin, and to proceed with caution.

But the woman didn't heed her own advice. She continued to take to the road like a bolt of lightning.

"Your son's not the only one who races cars, I see."

"This is the only kind of racing I do now, but there was a day…" She trailed off and said no more.

The vehicle ahead took the exit off the highway, before reaching Norcastle.

Sylvie banged her steering wheel. "He must've figured I would set up a blockade in town." She took the exit, too.

"So we're going after him with no backup?"

Sylvie glanced his way. "You're a smart man, Ian

Stone. Or should I call you Luke Spencer? You may have dyslexia, but you can read a situation just fine."

"It's Ian, and you're right. This has insanity written all over it."

THREE

"Preston, this guy's heading up to Mount Randolph. How fast can you get a team up there? Charney Road's about to end. After that, snowmobiles will be needed. He's in an all-terrain Jeep. He'll get a lot farther than I will."

"I'm on it, Chief, but I was already en route to the town line. It could be a while before I get to the garage and load up the sleds."

"Smitty, are you reading this?" Sylvie asked, hoping Officer Ed Smith was on the transmission.

"10-4. I'm less than a mile away from the garage. You'll have your sleds in fifteen, little miss."

"Roger that."

"Boyfriend?" Ian asked when Sylvie pushed her car's tires to grab the snow. Her gunman's taillights were long gone, but not his tire tracks.

"Who? Smitty?"

"You seem...close."

"Smitty's old enough to be my father...and filled the role for a lot longer than my real one did. Or at least, he used to."

"Used to? When did he stop?"

"When I applied for the former chief's position."

"Not supportive of his little miss?"

"Just not as supportive as he was for Reggie Porter. Reggie had been on the force for thirty years. He was qualified, but…"

"But?"

"But nothing. I took the test and got the majority of the town council's vote. End of story. They had their reasons for choosing me, and everyone's just going to have to get used to it. It's been two years, almost, and I'm a good cop."

"Something tells me you're as stoic as one of Virgil's duty-bound soldiers in his stories."

"I see you make good use of your audiobooks."

"For someone dyslexic they're an answer to prayer."

"You pray?"

"Everyone prays. Whether they admit it or not, there comes a moment where everyone calls out for help."

Sylvie had to agree. She remembered her moment like it was yesterday, even though it was fifteen years ago.

"The Jeep's off to the right, hidden behind those pines. Your lights just reflected off the red taillights."

"I see it. Good eye." Sylvie pulled to the left. "Stay down," she instructed and radioed her location. Using her door as a shield, she crouched low, her gun drawn and held at the ready.

The cold night wind whipped around her and through the empty tree branches.

"Come out with your hands up!" she commanded.

No response.

Sylvie glanced into her cruiser at Ian. Slowly, he shook his head. It was as though he'd read her mind and knew what she was about to do. Again, the man may have trouble with his letters, but that was it.

She made her move and stepped out from behind her door. Ian mumbled his dislike under his breath. Then she heard his boots crunch on the snow. She swung around and pointed back at the car.

He did the same to her.

Seriously? Did he think she was a rookie?

What did she expect? Guys liked the idea of her being a cop for about ten minutes. Just until she had to do her job and go into the danger.

Sylvie turned her back on him and approached the Jeep. She breached the pines and came up on the rear of the vehicle. With one hand, she grabbed her flashlight and shined the beam into the rear window. Through the back driver's side door, she peered inside.

No signs of life were evident.

"There're snowmobile tracks out here," Ian whispered loudly from the other side of the trees. "Whoever he is, he's long gone."

"Well, his Jeep won't be here when he returns. I'll have it processed for prints before the morning."

"Get away from the car."

Sylvie shined the light in the direction of Ian. "Excuse me? You keep forgetting this is what I do. I go in when *you* can't. I definitely don't take orders from you. I may have to protect you with my life, but the oath ends there."

"Get…away…from…the car!"

Ian's tone had Sylvie questioning her decision to approach the vehicle in the first place. Did he know something?

Slowly, she stepped back through the pines. His arms were around her so fast, lifting her frame off the ground and across the road. She barely had time to fight back with anything more than a few twists of her body when a flash of light lit the sky above and an explosion rushed at her from behind.

A painful ringing filled her head. It took her a few seconds to realize she was on the ground with Ian over her. His head of hair brushed her neck. Her gun and flashlight were gone to places unknown, her ears pierced with the effects of the blast.

Her lungs emptied in the toss. They burned with a need for air that Ian's weight didn't allow for replenishing.

Sylvie banged a fist on his back. "Can't—" she pushed out in a squeak "—breathe."

Ian moaned, but didn't move quickly enough for her. She banged three more times before his head lifted with a dazed look of confusion.

Had he lost consciousness? She couldn't assess him until she could breathe.

Ian snapped to and rolled off her, allowing air to enter her body. Heat roared at her from the fire across the road, fighting her for the oxygen. She heaved over in spasms.

"Easy. Slow it down. Breathe into your nose, not your mouth." Ian's soothing commands and his hand on her back told her he'd returned to her side.

But what about him? He'd taken the brunt of the blast. Was he burned?

Sylvie followed his directions but willed her lungs to fill enough for her to help.

"Let me check you out," she said on a breathy whisper.

"Just a little singed. The coat's trashed. I can feel wind on my back, and it actually feels good. I probably won't need a haircut for a while, either." He laughed, but she didn't think she'd heard such nervousness in him before.

"Just humor me and turn around."

"Fine, but I may not be decent." More nervousness threaded through his voice. He was scared.

But then so was she.

"The trees took the brunt."

Sylvie glanced at the flaming pine trees with the burning car behind them. The trees had saved their lives.

But Ian had saved hers by telling her to get away from the car in the first place.

"How did you know?" Her voice cracked.

She touched his obliterated jacket pieces, pulling them away from his body. His shirt stuck to him. He grunted when she lifted it.

"You're burned, but I don't think anything more than second degree in a couple spots. It'll feel like a bad sunburn."

"Thanks, Doc." Ian rolled and lay in the snow, gritting his teeth against the cold, but it seemed welcoming at the same time.

"You still haven't told me how you knew."

"Just a feeling of impending doom. I'm attuned to stuff like that."

"From experience?"

"You could say that. You face it enough times and you start to live on the balls of your feet, ready to spring into action or retreat, whatever comes first. Besides, it looked like a setup. Like I was supposed to find that car. Me. Not you. Regardless of your oath and duty you didn't sign up for this." He lifted up from the snow and leaned in close. "Leave me here. Go home to your son. I would never forgive myself if he lost you because of me."

"Because you're not worth me doing my job?"

Cruisers' lights and sirens blared off in the distance as they stared at each other.

"You shouldn't have come looking for me at my apartment."

"And find you washed up on the riverbank instead? I don't think so. Someone wants you six feet under, Mr. Stone. They're going to have to go through me first."

"You see the flames, right? The Spencers are your friends but with me around they won't think twice about leaving your son an orphan."

Cars rushed in and squeaked to a stop around them. As glad as she was to have their help, they could use this scene against her, especially if Preston was right in his thinking and somebody wanted her off the job. "Can you not tell them I approached the vehicle alone?"

Ian eyed her quizzically. "Aren't you the chief?"

"Yes, but I still have two more months on my probationary period and someone on the force may be looking for any slipup to stack against me. Please."

"Only if I get a sled."

"No way. You're going into protective custody. I can't allow you to go up the mountain with us."

"And I can't allow you to put yourself in danger for me."

"It's my job, Ian."

"Not for long if I tell them you approached the car without backup."

"That's blackmail. I can arrest you, you know."

Ian shrugged. "I'm always ready to spring into action, whatever that might be. In this case it will be your choice how this all goes down. So, what's your decision, Chief? Do I get a sled or do your weekends open up?"

"You could be killed," she said quietly.

"And so could you. Don't make me responsible for leaving your son alone in this world. I have to look myself in the mirror every day. You should know about mirrors more than anyone. You've made sacrifices to give Jaxon a good life."

His reference to her circumstances as a pregnant teen silenced her. He'd obviously done the math. However, she didn't feel his judgment like so many others. Just his understanding. She did what she had to do to look herself in the mirror every day. She couldn't take that from Ian.

"Chief!" Smitty fell to his knees beside her. His wisps of balding hair fell in his face. "Are you hurt?"

"No. I'm fine. Ian has lost his coat. Did you bring the winter gear? He'll need a set."

"A full set? Is he going up the mountain?" Smitty glanced Ian's way in confusion. Caution took over. "Who are you?"

"He says he's Lu—"

"I'm Ian Stone." Ian glared at Sylvie as he cut her off. "Just call me Ian, and everyone stays safe."

Sylvie realized the ramifications of having this knowledge. If someone was trying to kill Ian before Roni and Wade learned he was alive, they could come after her, too.

Protecting Ian was one thing, but as a single mother, making herself a target was not a road she could afford to go down.

"Ian's going up because he thinks he can ID the shooter," Sylvie told her men.

Ian nodded at her decision to allow him to stick by her. He really had no intention of getting her fired if she didn't comply, but he did intend to keep her alive. And to do that, he couldn't stay behind.

Sylvie jumped to her feet with rapid orders spilling from her lips. Her team responded on her command. When no one squabbled over her decision, Ian could tell they respected her as their leader.

One half of the team stayed to process the scene and wait for the fire department, while the other prepped the sleds and geared up.

As Ian pulled on his second glove and stamped his feet in the too-tight boots given to him, Sylvie pushed a helmet at his chest.

"Don't make me regret this, Ian. And make sure you stay alive." She climbed on her sled. "We ride!" Three of her officers fell in behind her. Ian straddled his sled and started the engine. He revved the gas by turning the handle and after getting acquainted with his machine, saluted Sylvie to let her know he was good to go.

She took off at a breakneck speed. She'd hinted at racing cars as a retired pastime, but obviously snow-mobiling hadn't been given up. Ian had trouble keeping up with her and her team. He had one officer behind him, pressing in on his tail. The guy didn't like lagging behind, judging by the way he pressed close. Ian gave his sled more gas and leaned in.

Still the officer hedged in.

The officers' helmets had radios installed in them so they could talk with each other, but no one had given him one. Yelling at the guy to back off did nothing. Ian couldn't even hear himself over the engines.

But he *could* feel the officer practically breathing down his neck. Ian's sled was already pushed to the max. What more did the guy want? Any faster and Ian would be on top of the officer in front of him. He pushed on, but finally couldn't take it.

Ian flashed his headlight to get someone's attention.

Only not one person ahead or behind responded with a word or hand signal. Not even a brake light to show they'd slowed down.

Was it a scare tactic done by the police? Was Sylvie in on this?

Ian's snowmobile jerked and skidded from an impact from behind. He'd been hit. He righted his machine, but knew the officer had struck him with his sled. This just went from annoying to…calculated.

But Sylvie couldn't be involved. Her oath of duty to serve and protect drove her every decision. The cop behind him was working alone…or perhaps was working for someone else.

The Spencers.

Their wealthy reach exceeded the local PD. They must have people bought and paid for in every back pocket of their designer jeans.

Ian craned his neck to catch a glimpse of the guy so determined to push him off course.

For what?

Was the shooter waiting for him nearby? Maybe this officer just had to roll Ian's sled off the path and let the killer finish what he was sent here to do.

Get rid of Luke Spencer.

Ian jammed the back of his sled out in a fishtail to push his pursuer off. He stood to his feet on the sled and ramped up the engine to catch up with the officers in the lead. His engine screamed at the assault. He cranked the handle harder, popping the front end of the sled up and back down with a thud.

His teeth jarred with the impact, then clenched as the machine blasted up the mountain. A quick glance over his shoulder and he found his tail gone. Ian drove on and quickly caught up with the other four officers.

The number stumped him. There had been three officers and the chief when they set out, and still there were three officers and the chief.

Then who had been trying to run him off the path?

Ian pushed on to reach the group. Something told him the guy they were pursuing had been behind him the whole time.

The assassin had made the tracks for them to follow, then circled back around to nab his assignment. But where were the tracks leading the police?

Trap. The word lodged in Ian's throat. He shouted it to no avail. They would never hear his warning before whatever awaited them made its appearance. With no radio, all he could do was race headfirst with them into a trap that Sylvie would fall into before anyone else.

Ian had to stop her. She was experienced, but in the dark mountain night, with only the lights on their sleds, her vision was limited to a few feet. Just enough to keep an eye on the tracks leading them to…where?

A dead end?

Sweat poured down Ian's back into his suit. His burns were nothing compared to the painful fear gripping his lungs in a vise. Sylvie didn't deserve this. *He* was the one who'd brought this danger to her town. *He* was the one they wanted, and they didn't mind killing a few cops to achieve their goal.

It wouldn't even look like murder. It would look like a horrible snowmobile accident that took the lives of four brave officers in hot pursuit. This guy was a skilled mastermind killer.

Ian pushed on, but realized he would need to leave the path and cut them off ahead. It would be the only way to stop them.

Ian peered into the darkness for an alternate path. When one off to his left came into view, he took it and brought his sled up and around a steep pass. At a point he had to stand and lean forward to prevent his sled from falling backward. Overturning it now would be catastrophic.

Finally, his path rejoined the other one, but Sylvie had already flown by.

Ian was able to pull out and cut the officers off.

Two collided at the shock of seeing him, not able to brake fast enough. The third officer pulled off to the side.

Ian whipped off his helmet. "It's a trap! The guy tried to take me out down the mountain. One of you, radio to stop her."

"Her radio's not working!" the one who had pulled off shouted. "We've been trying to get ahold of her."

Ian didn't wait for any instructions. He had to get Sylvie. He pushed his sled back into Drive and screamed it up the mountain.

Quickly, she came into view…but so did the end of the road. Ian's light took in all that surrounded her from this far back. But she would only see what was directly in front of her. What she was meant to see.

The tracks.

Tracks that were about to come to an end without warning—straight off the side of the mountain.

FOUR

Sylvie cranked her throttle to give her engine the gas it needed to continue its steep ascent. She tried her radio again.

No response. She risked a glance over her shoulder to catch her team's headlights. At least one kept up.

She slowed to allow the rest to do so and quickly the one sled pulled up alongside her. A gloved hand reached over and grabbed her hand.

"What are you doing?" she yelled inside her helmet. She didn't expect an answer. But suddenly the man pulled her hard and she lost her grip on the snowmobile. His assault didn't let up and before she could fight back, she found herself draped over his sled and veering in another direction.

The ride came to an abrupt end and Sylvie pushed off into the three-foot-deep snow, landing on her back.

The driver's hand lifted her up. Sylvie ripped away from him to go after her sled.

Only she couldn't see it. She also couldn't hear it.

She tore off her helmet and looked back at the man who'd removed her from her ride. She stepped up to his sled and hit the red kill switch. The machine shut down instantly. "Take the helmet off."

He did as he was told.

Ian's face appeared beneath the great unveiling.

"I should have left you behind," Sylvie said.

"Because I saved your life again?"

"How did you save my life?"

"Do you see your sled around? No, you don't. That's because it was a trap. You were following tracks that led you off the side of the mountain."

Sylvie whipped around to search the darkness for her snowmobile. Even if it had crashed and the headlight had gone out she would have seen evidence of it around. A dark abyss less than ten feet away could only be what swallowed it, and it would have taken her right along with it if...

"We weren't the ones doing the chasing," Ian said. "He tried to get me away from the pack a little ways back there."

She pivoted back. "While sending the cops to their deaths?"

"Looks that way. You should get as far away from me as you can before it's too late for you and your men. Go now. Leave me here. I beg of you."

"Be serious. I'm not leaving you up here. You'd die before morning, whether killed by this guy or the elements." Sylvie needed to do what their enemy wouldn't expect. Did he know these mountains? If she went left, she would pick up the McKeeny Pass and could cut down into inhabited land. There was also an emergency supply cabin at the beginning of the pass. But if she started on her way, it would be for the duration.

"You up for a ride?"

"I don't think this is a good time for an adventure."

"It's not a good time to die, either. I'm thinking our guy will be expecting us to double back. He'll be waiting to spring another trap for you. Christmas is two days away. I mean to be sitting around a tree sipping eggnog, and I'd like to do that without all the paperwork your death would heap on my desk. I'd also like to be alive to pick my son up from the hospital in the morning."

"So what's your plan?"

"I know another way down. We have to go across the McKeeny Pass. The ridge runs along for a few miles, then it descends to safety. You can trust me. I've driven these trails many times, but there's a chance we'll run out of gas and will need to walk the rest of the way. Are you too hurt for that?"

"I'm fine. Hop on."

"Wait, I need to tell my men."

As if on cue, the three of them cleared the slope. "Chief? Are you all right?"

"Karl!" Sylvie approached them. "We're not going down the way we came up. It's too risky for Ian. I'm taking him across the pass. Are you guys able to get back down?"

"We lost a sled, but we'll double up."

"Us too. I need you off this mountain as fast as possible. We're dealing with a psychopath who doesn't care if he takes you out in the process."

"Should we call Reggie?"

The name Reggie froze Sylvie's chest faster than the freezing temperature "No. There's no need to call him in. Let him enjoy his retirement."

"But—"

"No *but*s. Do not, I repeat, do not call Reginald Porter. We will catch this guy on our own. Now go."

Her men followed her orders, but she could tell they were hoping to call in the man who had been next in line for the chief position. She still had a lot to prove to her team. Sylvie hoped catching this guy and keeping Ian safe would be what it took to earn her rightful place as chief in their eyes. But even if it didn't, it wouldn't change the fact that she was still in charge.

Ian held on to Sylvie's waist as she pushed the snowmobile through deep snow. He kept an eye out behind him every few seconds to be sure they didn't have unwanted company. Two hours of riding at a slow twenty miles an hour, Ian worried they weren't putting enough distance between them and his would-be assassin. The guy knew how to use these treacherous drops to his advantage. Ian peered over the side of the ridge to his right. One push and they would be bouncing over jagged rocks all the way down. In addition to speed, he questioned Sylvie's choice of path.

The snowmobile slowed even more until it drifted to an idling stop. Sylvie hopped off and indicated a small cabin down the hill about a hundred feet. The snowdrifts covered the door to about a foot from the top.

Sylvie's short legs disappeared in the heavy snow as she made tracks to the building. She pushed through, breaking trail with all her strength.

Ian joined her and reached the door to help her scoop the drifts away in a flying flurry. The door opened inward with ease and a cold woodstove in the center of the one-room cabin greeted them.

Sylvie lifted the visor of her helmet. The fact that she didn't remove it completely told him this was a quick stop. He lifted his own as she went to a cabinet in search of something.

"Do you use this place a lot?"

"No, but I know it's stocked with things we might

need to keep going." She lifted two pairs of snowshoes from a rack.

"We're hoofing it from here?"

"This is heavy snow and not compacted down. It's causing the sled to use more gas than normal to get us through. I almost thought we wouldn't make it here at all."

"There's no gas here?"

She slammed a cabinet door then opened another. "Not that I can find. I'll make a note to have it stocked." Sylvie looped ropes over her shoulder. "When I was younger the McKeeny Pass was a place I would come to, to silence the world."

"Silence? Those sleds are the loudest things I've ever heard, and I work in construction."

She moved on to a drawer. "I guess the motor never bothered me, but I know there are people who hate it. Same thing with the racetrack."

"And yet that's not a part of your life anymore."

"Things change. Times change. Responsibilities change."

"Right, and your responsibilities dictate your days now, including protecting me. It doesn't matter how much you hate them."

"Hate is an emotion, and in this job there's no room for emotions. I make the best decisions I can with what is given to me."

"I've got news for you. I haven't been given to you, so you don't need to view me as one of your responsibilities to handle."

The whiny pine of a snowmobile drifted from the east.

"You're wrong. You're in my jurisdiction. I am responsible for what happens to you." She pushed the snowshoes into his arms. "Now let's move. That sled is getting closer."

Sylvie whipped her right-hand glove off and retrieved her gun from her holster. The .45 Glock consumed her small hand as she readied it to shoot. He closed the door as she led the way back to the sled. He dropped the snowshoes into the storage under the seat and waited for her to climb on.

"You're driving. I'm riding shotgun. Just follow the pass until it ends. If we make it that far, we'll stop and I'll give you directions from there. Pray that we do." With that she dropped her visor and communication ended.

Ian climbed on and started the engine. The gas gauge indicated less than a quarter tank. He closed his eyes and said a prayer to the only Father he'd ever had. The only Father who cared about him and promised blessings beyond Ian's imagination. Even when Ian didn't deserve them.

Ian hit the gas and moved across the pass as fast as the machine could get through the treacherous level of snow. He felt Sylvie grab hold of his waist with one hand and felt where she held her gun tucked against his back. But that meant her glove was still off. Her hand had to be freezing with the frigid cold and no covering, even held protectively between them. Would she be able to pull the trigger?

He pushed on so she wouldn't have to.

The only consolation was the assassin would be having just as much trouble getting through the elements as them.

The sled's high beam flickered and dimmed. The motor strained. The end of the road neared for them whether the pass came to an end or not.

Out of the corner of Ian's left eye, he saw movement come at them. His pursuer had found a faster way up here to cut them off. Ian yanked the sled to his left to cut in front of the other rider.

He gave the sled the last surge of gas to power them ahead. The motor screamed and the assassin's headlight came up on the right side. One shove over and Ian might be able to end this right now. But that risked sending them over the edge right along with him. Still, Ian had to lose the guy, but maybe breaking away wasn't the answer.

He let off the gas and pressed the brake controls, not enough to stop completely, but to slow down enough that the two sleds rode side by side. The two drivers looked at each other, their visors hiding their identities. Ian reached his right hand out as Sylvie's gun appeared over his shoulder aimed at the other rider. The hitman reached for the gun as Ian reached for the guy's kill switch.

The round red button that Sylvie had used on his own sled before depressed easily and shut down the machine, lights and all, in an instant. In the same moment, Ian kicked his foot out and sent the sled into a flip. The driver went flying over his handle controls and landed in the snow ahead of them.

Ian's machine puttered by him as the guy reached for them. *Please God, just a little farther to give us some space.* Ian managed to squeeze out enough gas for another few hundred feet. He moved the vehicle down to the left behind some trees and he and Sylvie made fast work strapping on their snowshoes.

They lifted their visors to talk. No need to whisper since the assassin's motor was back in full swing and would be coming up on them real soon.

"Do you know where we are?"

"Yes, but we have to keep moving. There's a home nearby."

"Someone lives up here on this mountain?"

Sylvie didn't reply and Ian took that as a sign to keep moving. They hoofed it for what could only be another mile. The sound of the motor ceased, which meant the guy either gave up his chase or was following on foot. Snow fell down on them, first a few light spattering flakes, but quickly Ian's visor required swipe after swipe. His fingers numbed quickly even in his gloves. A look to his left and he saw Sylvie still held the gun, her hand exposed. He reached for the gun and had to pry it from her hand. Not because she fought him, but because it had frozen to her skin. He took his own glove off and pushed her small hand into it. His would be warmer than the one in her pocket.

Ian pushed up her visor and witnessed pain on her face. She fought it with her every breath and averted her gaze to his right. A glance that way and he saw a rustling in some snow-covered shrubs.

A bear, perhaps? Great. If the killer and the snowstorm weren't enough, now they would have a preying animal on their heels.

Ian lifted the gun in his hand and took aim at a creature barreling at them full force. The animal bounced up and out of the snow, flying through a blinding flurry of whiteness. The rapidly falling snow made it impossible to tell what kind of animal had set their sights on them.

Ian could do only one thing.

As he pressed the trigger to unload the bullet, Sylvie steamrolled herself directly at him, sending them both sinking into the snow.

Ian quickly rolled over to protect her from the approaching threat. Figures the woman would want to protect the animal. "Do your responsibilities extend to protecting the creatures in your jurisdiction, too?"

The animal landed hard on Ian's back, putting its whole weight on him and not giving an inch.

Sylvie glanced over Ian's shoulder, her eyes wide.

"Is it a bear?" Ian asked low and controlled. Sweat beaded up on his forehead.

A giggle erupted from Sylvie, and Ian realized it was the first time he'd heard her laugh. It was the first lightheartedness he'd seen her express. Never would he think it would come out in a time of danger.

"Well, what is it?" he demanded.

She reached a hand up and lifted his visor. "It's Promise." Her lips curled with mischief.

"Promise? Promise what? Now's not the time to be making deals, Sylvie. Just tell me what kind of animal is on my back. Is it a mountain lion?"

"She just told you," a deep male voice spoke from above them. He sounded mad and lethal. Had his killer caught up to them? "Promise is my service dog, and you nearly killed her. That doesn't make us friends, just so you know."

Ian squinted into Sylvie's almond-shaped eyes. He knew them to be green, but without light all he could see was the glistening tears of laughter in them. "What's so funny?"

"Ian, meet Wade Spencer." She lifted her head and chinked her helmet against his. She moved her lips in a bare whisper. "Your brother."

FIVE

Stockings hung with embroidered names from the Spencer family's fireplace mantle, some old and worn, many new. Sylvie watched Ian study the long row before he gave his attention back to rubbing her pained fingers near the flame.

"I don't need you to do this," she said. "I can warm my own hands."

Ian rubbed on, glancing over his shoulder. She followed his gaze and saw they were alone. "Why did you bring me here?" he demanded. "They are the enemy. They're the ones behind ordering the kill."

"I wouldn't have brought you here if I believed that. They are good people."

His hands pressed harder. "Good people with money. That Christmas tree has to be pushing twenty feet." Ian jabbed his head in the direction of the elaborate holiday spruce reaching to the high ceiling of the Spencers' ten-thousand-square-foot home. He nodded to the long row of stockings. "Who are all these people? Do they all live here?"

"No." Sylvie pointed to the first two stockings in the line. "Wade and Lacey are married. She's expecting their first baby any day now. In fact I think she's over-due. But soon there'll be another stocking beside theirs."

Sylvie couldn't contain the excitement about the new arrival. She was so happy for Wade and prayed his new baby would bring healing to him just as Jaxon had done for her so many years ago. She wasn't the same person she was before, all because of a new life.

She pointed to the next stockings in line. "Roni is married to Ethan. They do live here. Ethan was an FBI agent and the FBI called him in to help with an un-dercover case for a few weeks. But Roni still has his stocking out, so maybe he'll be home for Christmas. Then there's Cora, who used to be the Spencers' maid, but she married their uncle Clay, making her official family, not that she wasn't already. She's lived here for forty years, long before their parents were murdered."

"My parents, too," he pointed out under his breath.

"Right, sorry." Sylvie moved down the stocking line. "Magdalena is a woman Roni freed from a human traf-ficker last spring. She lives here permanently now and also goes by the name Maddie. She helps Roni run a refuge here for women who've been trafficked, which leads to the next two names. Angela and Sarah were brought here after their captor was arrested. They're in protective custody while he's being prosecuted for his crimes."

"Will they stay here forever?"

"For however long they need to. If that's forever, then it's forever. Many of these girls feel they can't go home. Roni gives them a fresh start if they want it. She had a third girl who returned to her captor over the summer. It was hard for Roni to accept, but…well, it's just the girls are so broken, some of them don't know any other life, or don't feel worthy of a better one."

"I thought Roni ran a racing school. That's what her website says."

"I thought you couldn't read."

"My boss read it to me. He's the one who convinced me to come back here and accept my inheritance. I wasn't going to. I should have listened to my gut telling me this was a bad idea."

"This is the guy you work for in construction?"

"Alex Sarno of Sarno Construction, soon to be Sarno and Stone. He's promised to make me a partner in the business when I get back."

"But first you need to get your hands on the Spencer dough, is that it? Did he promise you this partnership before or after you told him the news of your birth family?"

"Does it matter?"

"Maybe, maybe not."

"I say not. Alex took a chance on me when no one else would. He's watched me struggle and has helped me rise above my circumstances. He took me to church with him. It's because of him that I know God wants more for me than to be an illiterate lackey for the rest of my life."

"That sounds great and all, but money does strange things to people. Makes them act differently. Selfishly."

"You think Alex is after my money?"

"You don't even have it yet, and the man already offered you a part in his business. Did he name a price, or is he eagerly waiting to find out what you stand to gain from the Spencers?"

Wade cleared his throat from the doorway. He stood there with Promise beside him, his hand in her fur at her head. "Stand to gain from us? I already don't like you for shooting at my dog. If it wasn't for Sylvie's quick reflexes, Promise wouldn't be here keeping me calm. But maybe I should be kicking you out of here anyway."

The golden Labrador retriever pressed her head deeper into Wade's palm.

"Wade has post-traumatic stress disorder," Sylvie said. "Promise is his service dog. She helps with his daily activities that his memories impair. You see, he's also had circumstances he's struggled with over the years. In fact, he turned his back on all you see around you for the life of a soldier. He knew money never fixed anything."

"Never." Wade stepped farther into the room, but the man's hard-edged tone had disappeared. He must have sensed Sylvie was helping Ian to understand something and Wade respected her to know her business. She felt safe from having to answer the question of who Ian was…for now. He was an army captain, however, and would want to be briefed about why they were out in the storm and running from someone.

She didn't know Wade well enough to know when he would require the knowledge, though. Roni was the closer friend, and even Sylvie's relationship with his sister hadn't come easy. Sylvie grew up downtown. Her family worked for the Spencers, and friendships between the kids would never have happened in polite society.

But polite society wasn't the natural way of things. Kids didn't care about the rules of social classes. They wanted to play, and on one of Sylvie's hikes up the mountain to the McKeeny Pass, she came into contact with a very rebellious Roni Spencer on her snowmobile. The teenager gained a friend she could break all the rules with. She taught Sylvie to ride the sled as well as the race cars. She even introduced her to the handsome racer, Greg Santos.

The charismatic man quickly took notice of the blond-haired, green-eyed nobody who worked the concession stand at the track, and quickly took advantage of her.

Sylvie had fallen hard. She couldn't believe Greg Santos would pick her over all the pretty, wealthier girls. Looking back, she had to think the other girls wouldn't have him because they knew something she didn't.

It wasn't long before she understood and found herself alone and pregnant. Sylvie's days of playing came to a screeching halt. From then on, playing consisted of baby rattles, stuffed bunnies and lullabies.

Something Wade would soon be enjoying, as well.

"How's Lacey? Is she here?" Sylvie strayed to safer conversation.

"I left her in town at Clay's. I don't want her on the mountain in case she goes into labor. The snow's getting worse by the minute."

"I'm sorry I took you from her, but we appreciate you coming out to meet us."

"With Ethan away undercover, I had to. Your team came straight to Clay's and told me you would be coming out on the other side of the pass onto our land. I didn't want Roni out there searching for you, although she would have gone, no questions asked. Who is this guy you're running from?" Wade asked the question to Ian.

Just as she'd thought. Wade wouldn't wait for answers.

But would Ian give them? The anger in his eyes said things could get ugly, especially since Ian believed Wade and Roni were behind the order to kill.

Ian looked to Sylvie, his lips tight. "I would like to know that, too, but at the moment, I'm in the dark."

So he was playing it safe. Smart man.

"Where you from?" Wade asked.

Ian replied, "California now. Washington State originally."

"What's your last name?"

"Stone. Ian Stone."

"Stone… Stone." Wade squinted as he looked to be contemplating something. "You have family around here?"

Ian pressed his lips even tighter. It had to be killing him not to say who he really was. "Somewhere." He locked gazes with Sylvie, and she offered a sad smile. Why didn't he just tell the truth? This could all be out in the open and dealt with tonight.

She decided to offer a lead in for Ian if he wanted to take it. "Wade, Roni told me earlier today that you had another man notify you about possibly being your brother, Luke. How'd that end up?"

Wade shrugged. "Just like the last one. We served him his walking papers. I thought he might need a little more persuasion of the full-contact kind to take his leave, but he saw reason by the end." Wade raised his fist. "Meet Reason."

All right, so maybe things wouldn't be all dealt with tonight as she'd thought. Still, the time would come when Ian would have to tell his birth family who he was. In the meantime, she just needed to do her job.

"We don't know who's after Ian. He thinks it's a hired gun to take him out."

"Did you upset someone you shouldn't have?" Wade asked. "Someone in the mob, perhaps?"

"CIA."

"That'll do it. I might be able to help. I have family in the CIA."

"I don't want your help," Ian responded forcefully.

Wade raised a hand in surrender. "Your choice. If you change your mind just let me know."

Roni swept into the room with a tray of snacks. She placed it on the square coffee table and flipped her fiery red hair, exposing the burn scars on her neck left over from the car crash.

Sylvie caught Ian staring at the raised skin in mute silence.

"What are you looking at?" Roni stepped toward Ian, her head lifted to show the scars. "Didn't your mother ever teach you manners?"

"Roni, don't start," Wade said. "You're just instigating a fight. You're used to people staring at your scars and have never put anyone on the spot before. Give the guy a break. He's being hunted down."

"I'm not surprised someone wants to kill him. He's rude."

Wade smirked at his sister. "Sounds like someone else I know. The two of you should get along great. Ian, help yourself to the food."

Ian curled his upper lip. "If she made it, I'd rather eat my shoelaces."

Wade nodded. "No truer words have ever been spoken. Just wait until you eat it."

Roni gasped and spun to face her brother. "Thanks a lot, Wade. I thought you were on my side."

"Why do you think I live in town? Since Cora married Uncle Clay, the cooking up here has gone downhill."

Roni pouted. "That's not why you live down the hill, and you know it. You don't live up here because—"

"Enough, Roni." The warning glare Wade sent his sister had everyone dropping their gazes to anything but the direction of the conversation. It had Promise burrowing her furry head into Wade's thigh and hand again.

Ian searched Sylvie's face for the answer to what had just deflated the room's atmosphere. She assured him with a slight smile that she would tell him later. It was good for Ian to see that his siblings suffered from the crash just as much as he did. They weren't the bad guys.

"You can stay here, Ian. You'll be safe." Wade brought the subject back on task. "The glass is all bulletproof. And the food really is not that bad. Especially when Magdalena cooks."

"I have my own apartment in town. At one of the old mills."

Sylvie put a hand on his forearm. "Actually, staying here's not a bad idea. I can't find this guy and protect you at the same time. You saw how that turned out tonight."

"You are not leaving me here," Ian practically growled at the idea.

"Not big enough for you?" Roni taunted.

"Not with you here," Ian responded.

Wade shook his head. "What is up with you two? Do you know each other?"

"We just met today," Roni said.

"Call it hate at first sight," Ian added.

Roni stuck out her tongue. "The feeling's mutual." She said it, but the sparkle in her eyes said she was having the time of her life sparring with him.

Sylvie puffed out an exasperated release of air. "Well, you two can have at it all night long while I get to work." To Ian she said, "Stay here. I'll be in touch in the morning."

"I'm going with you."

"Then it's a jail cell for you. That's the only way I'll know you're safe while I do my job."

"You need me to find this guy. He's a professional and won't show his face unless I show mine."

"I don't use civilians as bait."

A text beeped on Wade's phone. He read it and said, "This train is leaving the station. Lacey asked for pickles before I left. She's getting antsy. Am I bringing you two back to town?"

Sylvie warred within herself. All it would take was one wrong move to lose her job. Her probationary period was nearly completed, but it wasn't over yet.

A murder she could have prevented could end her future in an instant.

But where would Ian be the safest? With her in town, or up on this secluded mountain with Roni?

One look at Roni's scheming glare directed at Ian answered that question. Sylvie didn't think Roni was behind the murder attempts, but there was definitely animosity, and they could do each other harm up here alone.

"On second thought—" Sylvie grabbed Ian with her thawed hand "—he better come with me. A jail cell might be the safest place for him after all."

"You didn't even say goodbye to Wade. Pushing your brother and sister away won't help you," Sylvie said, as Ian noticed her cruiser in its parking spot in front of the station. Her men must have delivered it back. Snow covered the top by a few inches.

But where were the rest of the cars?

Ian scoffed at her words and brushed past her to reach the police station entrance first.

Sylvie's hand shot out to stop him. "You need to stay with me, Ian. I can't protect you if you go on ahead like that."

Now he really scoffed. "You're a foot shorter than me. You must see how ridiculous that looks."

"No, all I see is your dead body if I slip up."

The town's police station sported neon green trim around the top portion of the old building. It appeared to be an old car dealership from the 1940s, its art deco style still intact. Hard to take any of the Norcastle police seriously when they were holed up in this retrofitted building.

"Is there no one here? Who's watching this place?" he asked.

"Just the dispatcher. My team is still out," Sylvie said, shutting the door on the frigid night. "Carla, any word on tonight's events?" she asked a woman who sat at the front desk among a lighted switchboard and computer screen with a map of the area at her fingertips. She seemed to be in her sixties, brown hair cut short to the neck. So, Sylvie wasn't the only woman in the department.

"No, honey. But with the snow covering the guy's tracks, they're running out of options. I told them you called to tell me you made it to the Spencers' and were coming in. They'll wait for your direction from here."

"Did Preston join them?"

"Preston's still handling the Jeep that exploded. Trying to find its owner."

"He'll have a hard time. That thing is toast," Ian cut in.

Carla eyed Ian with a raised eyebrow. "Is this our victim?"

Sylvie entered an office with a large viewing window, likely the old car manager's office—now the office for the chief of police. "Ian Stone, meet Carla Brown," Sylvie hollered from her office. "She's been Norcastle's dispatcher since her late husband was chief two chiefs ago. And yes, Carla, Ian is our victim. I'm keeping an eye on him so no more bullets find their way into him. Any messages I should read first?" Sylvie lifted a stack of paper slips from her meticulous desk and flipped through them, tossing them one by one into the trash.

"Jaxon would say his." Carla cackled. "He called to say goodnight and wanted you to know he was sorry. I do love talking to that boy of yours. I should say young man now. He's growing up."

"Yeah, times are changing." Sylvie frowned through the glass. "Too fast."

"I know all about change. And I've learned to embrace it. Speaking of change, one of those messages is from you know who. He called with a few choice words about his wife leaving him. He's having a hard time accepting it, and I think he's figured out you know where she is."

Ian watched Sylvie bite her lower lip as she read the message. Her whole demeanor sagged. He wondered who you know who was.

Sylvie dropped the note to the desk. "Well, Carla, why don't you go on home? You don't need to hang around here while I answer these. Thank you for holding down the fort during tonight's escapade."

"Are you kidding? That was the most excitement I've seen since the shoot-out at the Spencers' last spring."

"Shoot-out?" Ian tuned in to the conversation. "Why was there a shoot-out at the Spencers'?"

"It had something to do with the men who kidnapped Roni. She escaped and they came after her," Carla offered as she retrieved her keys from the red pleather pocketbook on her scattered desk. She tightened her scarf and pulled the zipper of her coat up to her chin. "Those Spencers, I tell you, they're always being targeted for something. Such a shame. They're such nice people. Well, good night, all. Ian, nice to meet you. Stick by the chief's side and you'll be all right. She'll catch that guy after you. She won't sleep until she does."

The door closed on a gust of bitterly cold wind, and Ian turned back to the office window. He caught Sylvie studying one of the messages on the slips of paper. Her face darkened and she looked as if she were deep in thought.

"Is everything all right?" He stepped to her office doorway. She looked up as though she'd just remembered he was there.

"Um, yeah, everything's fine. Just a call from someone who used to work here. He wants to meet with me."

"And this worries you?"

"Worries? No. Yes. Maybe. Reggie Porter worked for the department for over thirty years. In fact, he worked here as a rookie the night the car carrying you and your family was pushed off the road."

Ian lifted his head. "Would he talk to me about it?"

"Are you going to tell him who you are?"

"Should I?"

"Why are you asking me?"

"Because if you don't trust him, I don't."

She paused. "I thank you for the vote of confidence, especially having only met me twelve hours ago, but yes, you can trust Reggie. Some days I wish the town council had awarded him the chief position instead of me."

"Why didn't they?" Ian stepped deeper into her space and dropped down onto the two-seater sofa. Sylvie dropped into her own chair and leaned back. She fit perfectly, as tiny as she was. She belonged in this room, and he had to think the council recognized this, too.

"Reggie had a heart attack, but that's between you and me. My men don't know about it. Reggie didn't want them knowing. He made up an excuse that he was taking the wife on an adventure in Europe, but really went to cardiac rehab. I guess he wanted to go out of his career with the guys seeing him still larger than life. I respect that, but…"

"But the guys think you stole the chief position from him."

Sylvie gave a sad smile and nodded. "Especially Smitty. I love the man. Have since I stepped into his church with my belly out to here." She modeled her pregnant belly with her arms extended as if she was trying to hug a snowman.

Ian chuckled. "I can't imagine you being that big."

"Oh, imagine it, buddy. There was no hiding a nine-pound baby."

"Nine pounds."

"And six ounces. You can't forget those six ounces."

"I wouldn't dream of taking away your thunder. Brag away, Mama."

She flashed him a beautiful smile. A row of perfect white teeth in a cherublike face. Her almond-shaped eyes crinkled at their edges. Her blond ponytail swung over her shoulder and rested there as she reached to toss the last of her messages on her desk.

"Who was Carla talking about? The man not happy about his wife leaving him."

Sylvie sized him up.

"You've trusted me with Reggie's heart condition. You must know I won't go blabbing," he assured her. It wasn't any of his business, but there was something inspiring about learning all that she handled in a day. Essentially keeping everyone safe.

"No town likes to admit they have domestic violence issues," she said. "They want to keep the persona of quaint little town, but even picturesque villages have their troubles. Let's just say I helped a woman escape hers."

"So you do know where she is."

"Of course. I brought her there." She smiled her bright smile of victory.

"Do you think Carla's right? Do you think the husband knows you know?"

"Doesn't matter. I will go to my grave with the location."

"What if he retaliates and comes after you?"

She barked with laughter. "Let him try. I won't need anyone pressing charges to arrest him then."

"Does Norcastle have any more of these domestic violence cases?"

Sylvie dropped her head to her chair with sadness in her eyes. He took that as a yes.

Ian not only saw all she handled in a day, but also how the situations she couldn't change affected her.

"I grew up in an abusive home, Sylvie. Don't be so hard on yourself. Some people are really good at keeping the law at bay."

Sylvie locked on his gaze. The anguish he saw in her

green pools didn't bring him comfort but he knew she wanted to fix his problem, too.

"It's done," he said. "But promise me you'll never give up going after the bad guys."

A liquid smile blossomed on her face. "Never."

"I wish I had a Chief Sylvie Laurent growing up." Ian took in her smile and thought about how stunning she looked relaxed against her chair. "But with all these guns aimed at me, I'm glad I have you in my life now."

"Speaking of which, you ready for your jail cell?" She unlatched her keys from her belt and swung the ring around her finger. Her face deadpanned.

"I think you're enjoying this too much. I hate to break it to you but I'm not going in your jail cell, at least not willingly."

She snapped her fingers with a dimpled smile. "Oh, fine, but that means I'm putting you to work." Sylvie stood and approached a filing cabinet. She rummaged through the top drawer and pulled out a paper roll. She unraveled it and draped it across her desk. A terrain map of a mountain lay before them.

"Is this the mountain we were on tonight?"

"Mount Randolph. Yes. It's also the mountain I think your gunshot came from. I'm thinking he's holed up here somewhere. He's spent some time on the mountain and knows the terrain enough to take out half my police department."

"Including the chief."

"I'm not any more important than my men."

"Jaxon would disagree."

Sylvie flashed him a heated glare from her hunched-over position. All sweetness gone. She jammed a pencil into her silky hair behind her ear and straightened. "You don't need to concern yourself with my son. We have a deal, a pact, which goes way back. He understands the dangers of my job. I don't shield things from him."

"He's still a fourteen-year-old boy with a single parent. Where's his father?"

"Again, none of your concern."

"No, but if you weren't around, would Jaxon's old man be back in the picture?"

Sylvie dropped her gaze to the map and pored over it with her full attention.

"Something tells me it wouldn't be a good thing." Ian pushed the conversation on, wondering more than ever who the man in Sylvie's life had been…and what would make him leave her and his son behind. The man must be insane.

Sylvie kept her head down and removed her pencil to circle a place on the map. "One more word out of your mouth, Ian, and I won't give you the choice about the jail cell."

"Just answer the question. Would you want Jaxon's father to be back in the boy's life?"

She threw the pencil down and came around the desk.

Ian stayed firm in his position, even when she grabbed his good arm and yanked it behind him. The woman had some muscle. He didn't doubt she could handle her own, but just as the incident on the mountain tonight proved, mistakes happened.

"Who's watching out for you, Sylvie?"

She paused in shoving him out the door. "I don't need anyone watching out for me." She jammed a hand into his back to make him move. They exited her office and walked across the hall to a metal door with a single window at the top. She opened it and pushed him inside. "Say hello to your room for the night."

She slammed the door, and he called out, "All this because you don't want to admit you haven't planned for Jaxon's future if something happens to you?"

He stepped up to the tiny window and watched her return to her desk to study the map. Her lower lip became something to bite on while she tapped her finger on the paper. She wrote something down on it, then took a picture with her phone. Ian figured she was working out a theory.

A movement off to the back of the department caught Ian's eye. The small window on the cell door blurred at the edges, so he couldn't get a clear view of what moved. But he didn't need to see who it was to know someone else was in the building, and they were keeping themselves hidden from view.

"Sylvie!" Ian yelled to warn her, not sure if he could be heard beyond the metal door. His room was probably soundproof.

The next second a gunshot blasted out in the bull pen and the window to Sylvie's office shattered into a million pieces.

Ian ducked out of instinct, but when he looked to her office again, she was gone.

The lights throughout the building shut down in a blink. Pitch blackness descended in the station. Even without the lights, it was obvious what was happening.

His would-be killer had returned. And there would be no kill switch to get them out of this one.

SIX

Sylvie's heart jumped in her chest, her breathing shallowed to quick gasps. She crouched low under her desk in the pitch black, fumbling for her gun at her belt. Sliding a round into the chamber, she debated her next move.

Get to the radio and call for backup. She could kick herself for not putting her individual shoulder radio back on when she returned.

And for putting Ian in the holding cell.

Did he know she hadn't locked him inside? She'd figured he would try the doorknob after she left and would show his annoyingly handsome face in her office any second.

Oh, how she wished he had. Then he would be next to her and she could protect him. How would she get to him in the dark with glass pieces to crawl over without alerting their shooter to her still being alive?

She had Ian to thank for that. If he hadn't called out her name in such a panicked pitch, she wouldn't have dropped to the floor. She would have been blown across her office before hitting the floor dead.

She had to get to him. She'd put him in there with no place to run. The shooter wasn't walking out of here without his mission accomplished this time. All he had to do was open the door and shoot Ian. A quick shot at close range. Job done. Ian was trapped…and she'd trapped him.

Sylvie reached her hand up to her cell phone. She'd placed it on her desk when she'd taken a picture of the drop-off on the map. The one she and her team had nearly plummeted over.

Quickly, she texted a message to Preston. Shooter at the station. Help.

She hit Send.

Please God, let there be coverage. Let this go through.

She couldn't wait for backup. She gingerly crawled out from her desk and patted the floor as she went. Two more steps and she exited her office for the wide open bull pen. She crawled two more steps and heard a loud crunch of glass beneath her knee.

A gunshot banged through the office and flew by her head just as she managed to fling her body to her left.

Sylvie's chest constricted. Her pulse tripped, then tripled in time. The bullet had come within an inch of her head.

A beep sounded from across the room. A phone lit up from one of the officers' desks. The light gave a quick shadowed depiction of the bull pen. A dark figure of a person appeared by Carla's desk.

Sylvie took aim and shot her gun three times toward where the figure had been standing.

The phone beeped again. The light now revealed no humanoid shadow.

The guy must have moved. She hadn't heard any- one fall.

She hastened to the cell, but when she reached the room, her hand hit an open door.

But who had opened it? Ian or the killer?

She looked to where she'd seen the shadowed figure. Had that been Ian? Had she shot him?

Loud breaths echoed through her head. She had to be alerting the killer to her location with every rush of air.

The front door burst wide and multiple flashlight beams infiltrated the dark. The back entrance also welcomed her backup. Preston had come through. Sylvie thanked God for getting her team to her so fast.

"I'm on the floor by the cell," she called out to them. "Ian Stone is in here somewhere."

And suddenly he wasn't somewhere, but beside her, pressing his head into her neck. "I'm right beside you." His arms engulfed her, and she returned the comfort with her own.

She couldn't stop herself. "Ian, I'm so sorry. Please forgive me. I shouldn't have put you in there. I shouldn't have let you leave my side."

"Shhh… I deserved it for sticking my nose where it didn't belong. I won't say another word about your son. You've done a great job raising him. You know what you're doing. Don't listen to me. What do I know? Nothing. I'm an idiot."

Sylvie shook her head and pressed closer to him, wanting to deny his remark, but also knowing she was unable to deny the fact that he had been spot-on about her lack of plans for her son if something were to happen to her.

The lights blared on overhead, revealing her team with guns drawn, but looking aimlessly around the office.

"There's no one here, Chief. The place is clean."

Sylvie released Ian and stood. But she stayed beside him. He offered his hand to her, and she held it tight. "Someone wants this man dead, and we cannot let that happen. It's going to be a long night, boys."

The cell phone on the desk beeped again.

"Which one of you left your phone here? I know we don't get the best signal up here, but you're still supposed to have them on you at all times."

"Sorry, Chief, that's mine." Preston stepped out from the rear of the room. His gaze jumped between Sylvie and Ian, a blatant question at their closeness in his eyes. But she had her own that took precedence.

"Yours? But I texted you for help. If your phone was here, how did you all know I needed you?"

Smitty raised his phone from his front pocket. "We all got the text, Chief. You must have sent a group text to all of us."

"I did?" Sylvie wasn't about to battle over silly matters. It was obvious she had, but in the darkness and in her adrenaline, she just hadn't realized she'd sent her message out to everyone. She sent a prayer of thanks to God for intervening. If she had sent the message to Preston only, he would have never received it, and she and Ian could be dead.

And Jaxon would be shipped off to Greg Santos.

Ian walked up to the hospital's front entrance with Sylvie guarding his back.

She spoke as the electric doors moved aside for them. "I've made arrangements for my neighbor, Margie Cole, to take Jaxon today. He won't like it, but I can't have him unprotected while this killer is walking around town and I can't have him with us."

Ian didn't like it, either.

"Your son needs you. If something happens to you because of me—"

"You need to accept my job as a cop, Ian. It's not going away, and I'm not, either."

They both wore bulletproof vests under their coats, but it still irked him to have her as his barrier to danger.

She peered over her shoulder to scan the horizon of the new day, but he knew she wasn't looking at the majestic beauty of the White Mountains.

She was looking for his shooter.

For what? To take the bullet for him? Ian shook his head in disgust.

"I hate you guarding me."

"I hate you doubting me."

Ian did an about-face "It's not about doubting you. It's about me being a man. I'm supposed to be able to handle myself, defend myself, but…" He stopped himself from sharing more than he needed to.

"That *but* is why I'm the one doing the guarding. I'm separated from this. It's got nothing to do with me and everything to do with you. Someone is after you. Someone doesn't want you making it home for the holidays. You're too close to this to be able to defend yourself. You're driving blind. Look at me as an extra pair of eyes. "

"And if my shooter strikes, getting you in the process, how do I explain that to your son?"

They walked to the nurses station and got Jaxon's room number. "I'll tell him right now so you won't have to."

"Great. Now a kid is protecting me." They entered the elevator and Ian hit the button for the third floor. "You really know how to make a guy feel less than adequate."

"But at least you're alive." She slapped a palm on his chest as the elevator doors opened to Jaxon's floor, stopping him from exiting first. Sylvie glanced down both sides of the hall before allowing him to move.

She kept her right hand over the gun on her waist as she walked. He knew her draw would be clean and quick if the need arose.

They reached Jaxon's room. She knocked and announced herself and Ian to her son.

The boy didn't reply. She pushed the door wide and revealed a man sitting in the bedside chair.

Sylvie fell back into Ian on a sharp exhale. Her fingers stayed over her gun. Ian knew this wasn't a pleasant surprise.

"Is everything all right?" he asked, reaching for her forearm for support, and suddenly he understood what she meant about the extra pair of eyes. Her ashen face told him she now was too close to this to make a good decision. She was too close, but he wasn't.

"Who are you?" Ian asked.

"Who are you?" the unknown man asked. It reminded Ian of his own encounter with a stranger in his hospital room in California a couple weeks ago.

But something told Ian this guy wasn't here to tell Sylvie she hailed from a rich family like *his* stranger had.

"I'm Luke Spencer," Ian said, knowing the Spencer name would hold a lot more weight than Stone.

The guy squinted, then flinched in confusion. The reaction was enough to give Ian the upper hand. "Luke Spencer's dead." The man slowly stood.

"So I'm told, but as you can see, I'm alive and well. I won't be able to say the same for you if you don't tell me who you are."

"He's Greg Santos," Sylvie answered for him, but the name meant nothing to Ian.

"What she means to say is I'm Jaxon's father."

Sylvie stepped in like a bulldozer. "You are not his father. Where is he? What have you done to him?"

The door behind them opened and Jaxon stepped in on quiet, unsure steps with his crutch. "He didn't do anything to me. I'm right here. I was in the bathroom getting ready to leave."

"With him?" She pointed to Greg.

"No, but I didn't know when you were coming. You didn't call to tell me."

"I couldn't, I was—"

"Yeah, I get it. You were working," Jaxon said and went to his bed to retrieve a department store bag. His outfit of blue jeans and red flannel was brand-new, the tags freshly torn and scattered on the bed. Ian figured dear old Dad had brought them as a bribe gift.

"Jaxon, your mom—" Ian started to explain why Sylvie couldn't make the call, but she cut him off with another palm to his chest.

Jaxon hefted his bag over his shoulder. He brought a winter cap down over his bandaged head and headed for the door, hardly in a rush with a boot on his broken leg.

Sylvie glared Greg's way. "You are not to go anywhere near my son. I will arrest you myself if you do. Pack your things and get out of this town."

"I plan to, but when I do, Jax will be with me, and there's nothing you can do to stop me. He's already told me everything I need to prove you are unfit to raise him, caring more about your job than our son."

"He's not your son," she repeated low and deadly.

"Saying it doesn't make it so. I've stood back long

enough. But now the boy needs his father, and I plan to be there."

Greg pushed past her with little effort, but Ian stepped in to block him. He had to look down to meet Greg's eyes. "You have no idea what you're getting into. I can go for years in court. I can make you wish you never stepped foot in this town. Better get yourself a good lawyer, because you can be sure mine will be top-notch."

Ian let him go by, but not without brushing against his shoulders. The guy was short, but strong.

The door shut and Ian asked, "What does he do for a living?"

Sylvie breathed deep and slow. "He races cars. He's pretty successful. Stood in many winner's circles."

"Meaning he's rich."

Sylvie's lips trembled. This was the first time Ian had seen fear enter her eyes since the moment the first gunshot went off. "He's won many purses. What he's done with his money, I have no idea. I've never wanted any of it, but I'm sure he can last a lot longer in court than I can."

Ian placed his hands on the sides of her face. "But is he Spencer rich?"

She gave a slight shake to her head, her eyes questioning where he was going with this.

"Then don't worry. You will not lose your son to that man."

"How can you say that? I can't afford an attorney and neither can you."

"Ian Stone can't. But Luke Spencer can."

SEVEN

Sylvie pulled into the driveway of her tiny row house in downtown Norcastle. The houses were all the same with their single floors and one-car carports. Typically, Jaxon's Legends car earned the shelter, but with his smashed-up car sitting in a garage at the track, she pulled her cruiser up under the carport and put it into Park.

Jaxon sat in the backseat behind the glass partition. His choice. He'd gone for the back door at the hospital without a word. He'd yet to say anything. The crack that had been growing between them widened into a wedge, shifting Sylvie's world. Ian placed his hand on hers and squeezed. As much as she appreciated his comfort, she couldn't let Jaxon see the intimate touch. She quickly removed her hand and stepped out of the car.

She came around to the passenger side and opened the rear door. Jaxon was unable to get out without the back door handles and would also need her help with his broken leg. Sylvie extended a hand to him. "Go to your room and grab a few things. You'll be staying at Mrs. Cole's tonight."

Instead of taking her hand for help, Jaxon pushed her away.

On a gasp Sylvie recoiled at her son's unusual response. Sure, lately he'd been growing distant, but never rude. She glanced at Ian and wondered if her son had seen him take her hand. He couldn't have with the closed middle partition blocking his view.

A need for the comfort Ian offered came rushing back. *No, not comfort.* She was losing her son right before her eyes and didn't know how to stop this growing chasm.

Ian stepped out of the car and insinuated he wanted to try. Why he thought he, a complete stranger, would be successful where the boy's mother failed boggled her mind. But she let him pass.

"I once had my shoulder torn from its socket," he said to Jaxon. "My right one no less, the same one that took the bullet. So if you don't mind, I can offer some help, but it's got to be from my left arm. Go easy on me. I can't have two bum arms."

"What happened to your arm?" Jaxon asked as he let Ian lift him from the backseat of the car. "Was it a fight?"

They hobbled up to the back steps. "Why? Do I look like the fightin' kind?" Ian smiled down at her son, and something in Sylvie stirred at the sight…and then quickly turned to a nauseating roll. She slammed the door on the idea of a man in either of their lives. They'd come this far without one, and they would continue as so. It didn't matter if the man's smile did funny things to her, or his hand brought on a semblance of peace. Those things were all temporary. Soon after he would try to change her…like so many other people. She said in a gruff, perturbed voice, "I'll go tell Mrs. Cole we're here."

No response came from either of the boys. As they

went inside the house, the two talked amongst themselves about how Ian had injured his shoulder. She doubted he was telling the truth when Jaxon laughed about an elephant playing a part in the fight.

Sylvie took a step toward her neighbor's house. It had matching yellow siding because Sylvie had gotten a good deal on the paint when she bought it off the Oops return shelf at the hardware store. She and Jaxon had spent the summer painting both structures, prettying up the neighborhood one house at a time, they'd said. Come spring they planned to plant pansies in the flower boxes. Or would it only be her...?

"Sylvie?" Ian had stepped back outside and now stood at the back door.

"Get inside the house where I know you're safe." The words came out clipped and angry, but didn't the guy realize the danger?

"Are you sure it's safe? Because someone's left you a message on your bathroom mirror."

"A message?" In confusion, Sylvie took two steps toward him. "What kind of message?"

"Jaxon found it. It says 'I found her.' Do you know what that's supposed to mean? Do you think it's a message from you know who about his estranged wife?"

Sylvie's stomach dropped like a heavy-handed fist. *He found her? But how?* Who had given up the location?

"Who wrote it? Sylvie, answer me! He was in your house."

Sylvie snapped her head up when she realized Ian had left the steps and stood in front of her. His hands gripped her shoulders, bringing her back to the present danger.

"You shouldn't be out in the wide open like this," she

mumbled about Ian's situation while her mind worked on someone else's. Would she be too late?

"Forget about me and tell me what's going on."

Jaxon stepped out the door, fear on his face, and she realized her son could have been hurt. What if he had been home alone when Clemson came? She thought she could do this job and keep Jaxon out of it.

She rushed to the door and wrapped her arms around him. She held on for a few moments and noticed he did the same this time. They may be growing apart, but they weren't broken, yet.

"Jaxon, I need you to go to Mrs. Cole's and stay inside until you hear from me."

She helped her son down the steps, trying to take it slow while danger pressed in faster than she could respond. She pulled him along, wondering how long that message had been there. Yesterday? Last night? This morning? *Please God, let it be this morning.*

"Why do I have to stay inside? I'm not a baby. I don't need to be watched. Does this have anything to do with Bret Dolan?"

Sylvie tripped in the snow and stared at him. "What do you know about Bret Dolan?"

"I know you're butting into his family. He's been harassing me for weeks about what you're doing. He says you're trying to take away his mom."

"I would never do that. It may look that way, but... Forget it. I don't expect you to understand."

"I would if you actually took the time to tell me." Jaxon limped away on his crutch, crossing the yard to Mrs. Cole's. The elderly woman opened her front door and waved to Sylvie, helping the boy inside as best she could. The woman wouldn't be able to do much to protect her son. A strong wind could take her down.

But Sylvie would have to take what she could and trust God to step in. She turned back to her cruiser and noticed Ian still standing under the carport.

Frustration whirled in her. "Didn't you hear me? It's not safe for you to be standing out in the open."

"And I said, forget about me."

"I can't forget about you. I need to keep you safe. It's my—"

"I know, your job. I get that. You're devoted to your job."

She reached her driver's side door. "Just get in," she told him, still not sure what she planned to do with him.

"Where are we going?"

"You can't come with me." She backed out of her driveway and knew where she could take him. "You're going to your brother's."

"Wade? But where are you going? To the woman you helped?"

"Yes. I pray I'm not too late. That message tells me her location has been found. She's in danger."

Sylvie hit her radio on her shoulder. "Carla, you read?"

"Go ahead, Chief."

"Has anyone reported a disturbance over at Evergreen Haven?"

"Nothing's come in." Sylvie let a little sigh of relief escape her lips as she drove. "Do you want me to send a car over?"

"No, I'm heading there now. But I do need Karl to get over to my house and process it for a break-in. I had one this morning."

"10-4."

Next she called Wade, but no answer told her taking Ian there was out of the question.

"You don't have to worry about me telling anyone where this place is," Ian spoke over her thoughts of a plan B. "I wish I had such a place to go to when I was young."

Sylvie let the rest of her stress go in the heavy silence. She remembered him saying he came from an abusive home.

She looked to his shoulder, the one he'd told Jaxon had been injured by an elephant. "So the shoulder was no circus accident."

He laughed a sad laugh and shook his head. "Never been to the circus."

She swallowed hard as she made up her mind. "I suppose if he's found her, then the secret's out."

"Who is he?"

"Ben Clemson. He's a mean drunk. I'll need to find another place for his wife, but I'll also have to find another safe house. It won't be a safe place for anyone anymore. Just when I was so close to helping another woman leave her abusive situation."

"The other domestic violence situation you mentioned?"

She nodded as she raced on.

"Who? This Bret Dolan that Jaxon was talking about?"

Sylvie glanced his way. "Bret Dolan's mother. She called me late one night from a pay phone in town, saying she'd left and didn't know what to do. She feared for her life and begged me to help. I picked her up and brought her to the station. She didn't want to go to the hospital. Carla and I helped her with her injuries. But then I pushed her away. I rushed her."

"How?"

"She allowed me to photograph her injuries. All I

wanted to do that night was go after Shawn Dolan and cuff him. I must have let it show too much. I tried to get her to press charges, and before I knew it, she was out the door. It was all too much for her."

"She went back to him."

Sylvie nodded. "Many times they go back. But I know she'll call me again someday, and this time, I'll have Evergreen Haven, a place to bring her to that would help her heal. Or would have, if Ben Clemson hadn't found the location. He'll tell everyone who will listen now, and I'm sure Mayor Dolan will be first in line."

"*Mayor* Dolan?"

"Affirmative. Bret's father is the mayor of Norcastle, and his wife's abuser. Told you, don't let the quaint little town fool you. Even Norcastle has ugly secrets."

"And you know them all. Are you sure you don't have people gunning for you, too?"

Sylvie took the turn into a campground that looked closed for the season. Cold little cabins dotted the hills that could be seen from the road, but as she drove farther into the property away from the traffic, he saw a large log cabin's chimney spurted smoke out the top. Beyond it, a red covered bridge gave access to the other side of the cold river that ran through town.

"It's peaceful here. You picked a good spot," Ian said.

"The bridge is a favorite spot. Jaxon and I have spent years walking to it for spring fishing, or for just thinking. Spending long hours here got me thinking that Evergreen Haven Campground would make a great location for a safe house."

"And only you and Carla know?"

"There are a few of my team who know. The ones I know I can trust. Now you."

Sylvie parked the cruiser and opened her door. "Stay here."

Ian opened his door and stepped out.

She sent him a frustrated look. "Fine, but if your presence makes anyone uncomfortable, I'll need you to back off."

"Got it."

They walked side by side up the front steps. Ian immediately saw the front door had been kicked in and stood ajar. He shot an arm out to stop Sylvie.

"We're too late," she said and reached for her radio at her shoulder. "Carla, I'm going to need that team over here. There's been a breach."

Sylvie drew her gun. She took a step toward the threshold, but Ian pulled her arm back.

"I'm a cop. This is what I do. I go in."

"You should wait for backup."

"You should wait in the car."

Neither of them was planning to follow the other's orders.

He trailed her inside, watching her back. She held her gun pointed up as she peered into the kitchen, her back to the wall. She entered and Ian stayed in the doorway to stand guard. He could hear something clicking. A door opened and closed before Sylvie returned.

"The stove was on. This just happened."

"Which means the perpetrator could still be in the house. We need to exit until backup arrives."

Sirens off in the distance grew closer. A creaking sound from above blared louder in his ears. Someone moved upstairs.

"Go outside, Ian."

He shook his head, giving her a taste of his stubbornness. He wasn't leaving her side. "Consider me an extra pair of eyes."

Her own words thrown back at her seemed to do the trick. She waved her gun for him to move away from the stairs. He stood behind her as they approached the landing. She took the first step in silence, then another and another. At the top, she turned to put her back against the hallway wall, pointing the gun for Ian to do the same.

Together they slid down the hall and entered a bedroom.

From their standing point the room appeared empty. Ransacked but empty. Sylvie checked all corners then walked over to a rug and pulled it up off the floor. Except it wasn't only the rug that came up. A door in the floor did, too.

She placed a finger to her lips and closed the door. She brushed past him and whispered, "She's safe."

Ian looked at the trap door and realized Mrs. Clemson was inside, hiding from the intruder.

He heard the downstairs become a bustle of cops storming in from all entrances, but Sylvie moved on to a second bedroom.

"Freeze!" she yelled.

A gunshot went off and Ian watched her go down with a thud.

"Sylvie!" Ian fell to his knees and crawled over to her. His body iced over instantly with a fear he'd never experienced before. He pulled her out into the hall, but she pushed him away. He reached for her again, needing to know she wasn't hit.

She reached for her shoulder radio. "Perp went out the back bedroom window upstairs. He slid down the roof. He's wearing a black ski mask, and army green clothing. About five foot eight."

"We heard a shot. Are you down?" came the response.

"Missed. Now find him."

Ian dropped his forehead into his hand on a sigh of relief. A groan escaped from his panting chest. "Are you sure you're okay? You're really not hurt? Not shot? You scared me half to death!"

She jumped to her feet, carrying on as though he wasn't having a heart attack and she hadn't been in danger of losing her life. It was business as usual.

She scanned the overturned room. "This place is a mess." Ian realized Sylvie wasn't going to allow him or herself to lose focus. He didn't know how she cut herself off from feeling fear right now, but if he meant to help her, he would have to follow her lead. He pulled himself together for the task at hand.

"The guy was looking for something," he said through rapid breaths.

"Someone." She lifted her chin to the other room. "His wife."

"I don't think so. He spent more time foraging than looking for the woman."

"We'll start with her husband. If he has an alibi that checks out, then we'll look elsewhere. The only thing I do know now is the place is compromised." She stood and walked back to the other room.

"And don't forget the part about nearly being shot. You could have been killed," Ian said, on her heels. "If the shot had hit you in the head, you'd be dead."

"Telling me things I already know won't help us catch this guy." She hit her radio. "I need the 411, guys. Have you caught him?"

"He had a snowmobile tucked in the trees. He's long gone. We'll get the sleds, but he'll still have a pretty good lead on us. What do you want us to do?"

"Not another sled chase, that's for sure. Let him go. We'll get him with a warrant. I want an alibi for Ben Clemson."

"Ben Clemson? His wife recently left him. He's been down, but why would you think he would break in here?"

"Because she was living here."

No response came, and Sylvie let them chew on that. She clicked off and stood. "Don't worry, Ian, I'm still looking for your shooter, too."

"My shooter, abusive spouses, your ex-boyfriend here to take your son. At what point do you reach your limit?"

"My last breath."

Ian sighed as she swept past him to help Mrs. Clemson from her hiding place. "How did I know you were going to say that?"

No reply came because Sylvie was giving a hand to two frightened women stepping out of the floor. Her soothing words caught him unaware. Her typical authoritative voice ceased in the presence of the ladies.

He followed them out to the cruiser. He overheard the second lady say she was the home owner when she walked over to an officer to give him her statement. Mrs. Clemson climbed into the rear cruiser seat. Ian got in the front and Sylvie assured her he could be trusted.

Ian faced the frightened woman. "I'm sorry you've had to make this decision in your life, to leave everything behind in order to survive. If it's any consolation, I grew up in a home with an abusive father, and I wish my mother had known someone who could help her escape. You're blessed to have Sylvie."

The woman lifted sad eyes, but she nodded her agreement. "I am so thankful to her. Before she became chief, I never believed I could be safe. She saw me one day and just knew I needed help."

Ian glanced Sylvie's way, astounded at the amount of compassion this small woman offered to so many. Some people were all talk, but Sylvie wasn't afraid to get her hands dirty.

They drove in silence all the way to a shelter two towns over. Sylvie walked Mrs. Clemson inside to get her situated and returned deflated.

"I hope she'll be okay. This isn't my jurisdiction. I can't protect her here." She pulled out onto the street to head back to Norcastle.

"How did you recognize the signs?" Ian asked. "Did Greg hurt you? Because one word and his case is over." Ian mumbled under his breath, "His life just might be over, too."

"No. Even if he did I would have a hard time proving that. Yes, he left me pregnant, but he never hit me. But his abuse was more about his lack of respect for me. I think that's what I recognized in Mrs. Clemson and even Andrea Dolan. They're not valued by the men in their lives. When I see that, I take notice of what's not visible."

"How has it affected your relationships since Greg?"

"There haven't been many. I went out a few times when Jaxon was six. I thought I was doing him wrong by not having a male figure in his life, but the men didn't understand my goal of being a cop. At first, it's exciting for them, but then they start wanting to change me. To keep me safe at home. They don't understand that's not me. It's like they can't handle what I do. So Jaxon and I made our pact that it would be just the two of us, and we would be enough for each other."

"You never dated again?"

"No reason to."

Ian found her remark to be disappointing. He didn't know why, but perhaps it was because Sylvie had so much to offer. So much love and compassion and companionship. It wasn't just someone else missing out on receiving all she had, but she herself was on the losing end, not receiving that love in return.

Especially when she gave it so freely.

"Well, I'm sure Mrs. Clemson will always be thankful to you. You didn't just change her life—you believed her."

Sylvie searched his face in the darkness of the car's interior. With night falling, they were ensconced in uncertainty. Uncertain of what was around them outside. Uncertain of what was happening to them inside. All Ian knew was Sylvie hadn't just changed those women's lives—she'd changed his.

"How many people didn't believe you, Ian?"

He looked out the passenger-side window. "Too many to count. Honestly, I think my dad paid the police off. I don't know how he came up with the money, because we lived in a small cabin in the woods and he never worked, but he always had money."

"What about your mom? What happened to her?"

"She died of cancer when I was seventeen. As soon as she took her last breath, I was out of there. If I'd had someone like you to call, maybe things would have been different. What you're doing—"

"What I'm doing could get me fired. Carla covers

me, but the town might not take too kindly to my clandestine efforts on their dime if they find out."

"But you're helping members of their town."

"Some might also say I'm breaking families up. There are some people who didn't like that I was a single mom, and it had nothing to do with the extensive duties of the job. That's why the council put me on a two-year probation. To give me ample time to prove I could handle the job. They weren't all for hiring me."

"I'll go out on a limb and say Mayor Dolan was one of them. Am I correct?"

Sylvie eyed him. "You're a smart man, Ian. You'll make a good Spencer."

Ian faced forward, unsure of how to respond. A smart man? That was a first. As for making a good Spencer, that was still up for debate. He didn't think he would even come close.

EIGHT

Sylvie pulled up to Clayton Spencer's prestigious Victorian home. Roni and Wade's uncle's sprawling house sat high upon the hill overlooking the town. The last time Sylvie had been here was last year for an intruder call when Wade and Lacey were in some danger of their own.

Lights glowed from all the windows, so Sylvie brought her cruiser to the gate and hit the button on the intercom.

"Is there a problem, Chief?" asked Clay when she stated her name.

"I need to see Wade if he's in."

"Yes, he's here. Roni's here, too. Lacey's in labor and everyone's hanging out. I'll open the gate. Come on up and join in the excitement."

Sylvie glanced Ian's way. "If you don't want to go up, we don't have to. We can head back to the station. There are officers there and you'll be safe. I won't let another breach happen."

"I say let's get this over with. With the whole family here, I'll be able to watch for the person who's out to kill me. Keep your enemies closer and all that."

"I wouldn't be bringing you here if I thought for a second one of them ordered the hit on you."

"Good friends, are they?"

"Only Roni."

"Then how can you be so sure?"

"I just know how much pain Wade and Roni have been through and how much they really want to put their family back together."

"And Clay Spencer, too?"

Sylvie paused to think about that. "Actually, I can't answer about him. The little bit I know isn't good."

"Like what?"

"Like he was friends with the man who had your parents killed. He says he had nothing to do with the murder, but there aren't too many people left to negate that."

"So what you're saying is Clay Spencer could have actually gotten away with murder. Did he gain anything from it?"

Sylvie drove up the curving driveway that encircled the property. Ornate lanterns lit the way, showcasing a stately home with huge wraparound porches and Victorian turrets signifying Norcastle's closest thing to royalty.

"Let's just say it was your mother who brought the money here. Your father and his brother, Clay, grew up downtown." She thumbed over her shoulder to point to the brightly colored Christmas lights down in the village storefronts. "And it didn't look like it does now. The factories closed up and most everyone was out of work."

"How'd my parents meet?"

"That would be a question for your family." She shut the car off. "But first you have to tell them who you are."

Ian opened his door and stepped out.

She rushed to his side. "You are supposed to wait until I come to your side. This place may seem secure with the gate, but I know for certain those barriers have been breached before, and could be again."

She had her gun out and they stepped up onto the porch. The door opened with Roni on the other side.

Her beaming smile died a fast death when she caught sight of Ian. "Don't tell me we're stuck with *him* again."

"Does it look like I'm coming willingly?" Ian thumbed over his shoulder at Sylvie. "She's got a gun."

"Will you two stop it?" Sylvie pushed Ian through the door Roni held wide. "I thought this would be the safest place right now. Even the station didn't sway the shooter. He broke in last night and nearly killed him."

"When she says *me* she means *her*," Ian corrected. "He nearly killed her."

Roni reached for Sylvie. "Are you serious? You were nearly killed because of this guy? Are you sure this is worth your life? What about Jaxon?"

"That's what I said," Ian said before Sylvie could state her pledge about serving and protecting. "It looks like we agree on something."

"That you're not worth her losing her life?" Roni said pointedly.

"Yeah, that too."

Roni's eyes squinted in speculation, but before she could retort, a man Sylvie had never seen before stepped into the doorway. Voices could be heard beyond him.

"It looks like we're barging in on a party," Sylvie said, ready to retreat to do this another time.

"Yeah, the whole family's home for Christmas. It's just perfect that Lacey will have the baby, too." Roni turned and smiled at the older gentleman in a black suit, his white hair neatly trimmed. "This is my grandfather."

The man offered a hand. "Chief Laurent, I've heard remarkable things about you. You go above and beyond your call of duty. I'm Michael Ackerman. Thank you for keeping my grandson safe."

"Your grandson? What are you talking about?" Roni asked, casting glances back and forth.

Michael smiled, his gaze on Ian. "Come in, Luke. We've been waiting for you."

Sylvie nudged Ian to move, but as he passed by Roni, her mouth hung wide in shock. Roni's sharp tongue had been officially silenced.

They all joined the group in the living room. Roni followed and took a seat. Her hands gripped around the chair's edges.

"Roni? What's wrong?" Wade asked his sister. She was growing as white as the snow starting to come down outside.

She stared at Ian, her eyes glued to him. She answered on a whisper, "Luke's come home."

"What are you talking about?"

Michael stepped up to Wade and put a hand on his grandson's shoulder. "What she's trying to say is your brother has been found. And he's decided to rejoin the family."

"Who said anything about rejoining the family?" Ian spoke up. "I'm here for one thing only. You told me I had to come back to claim my inheritance. So here I am."

Sylvie sighed and rolled her eyes. "Couldn't you have said that a little nicer? How about at least a 'Hello, I'm your brother. How've you been?'"

"And give these people another opportunity to take me out? I don't think so. And don't tell me they're innocent. You can't be totally sure someone in this room didn't hire the assassin out there. You can't be sure it wasn't one of them that nearly killed your team on the sleds and shot at you at the station."

Sylvie looked around the room. To Michael, Wade, Clay, even Lacey, who gripped her extended belly and breathed through a contraction as quietly as she could. Her dark brown hair was pulled back in a messy bun, but that was typically how she styled it on a regular day.

Sylvie looked at the clock and took note of the time. 11:20 p.m.

"All right," she said, removing a pad of paper from her belt. "If we're going to do this the hard way, I'm going to need to know where each of you were between eleven o'clock last night and five this morning."

The whole room broke into chaos. Shock turned to anger. But what surprised Sylvie was no one was angry about giving alibis for their whereabouts. They were angry that someone was trying to kill Luke Spencer.

Lacey whimpered from her spot on the sofa. Another contraction came swiftly. Sylvie glanced at the clock again. 11:22.

Sylvie slapped her notebook closed. "We'll have to pick this up later. Lacey, those contractions are two minutes apart. You're getting a ride in my cruiser." Wade and Ian jumped to. The two men stared at each other as they helped Wade's wife outside.

"Everyone else can follow," Sylvie said.

A dog barked and Sylvie realized Promise had been at Lacey's side. The golden retriever bounded for the door.

"Of course, you can come, too," Sylvie told her and rustled Promise's soft, clean coat of fur as they exited out into the falling snow.

Ian sat across the waiting room from his birth family. He fought to ignore their excitement, but found his lips twitching into a smile every so often.

"It's okay to be happy for them," Sylvie said beside him. "They're about to have an addition to their family."

Ian angled high eyebrows on her, waiting for her to grasp what she'd just said.

"Ian, there's room for more than one addition."

"They're trying to kill me to keep me out. Or at least one of them is." Ian studied Michael. The old man came from wealth. Ian was a penniless, illiterate construction worker. Why would Michael even contact him? The man was in the CIA. He had to know what Ian did for a living, the trailer he called home. The Spencers kept their cars in better places than where he lived.

Ian looked to Clay.

Sylvie said he didn't come from money, but earned it later in life. No, not earned, but inherited. He was no different than Ian. In fact, he would know exactly where Ian had come from because he'd been there. Just what would the man do to keep from returning to that destitute life?

The uncle's wife, Cora, held his hand. Ian wanted to know how the family's maid fit in with the family. Roni seemed to love her, judging by the way she hugged her repeatedly. But Ian figured if Clay raised Wade and Roni after their parents' deaths, then perhaps Cora filled a motherly role for them. But Ian wondered if she'd come into money because of Bobby's and Meredith's deaths, too. So far these two could have the most to lose.

"It's a boy!" Wade ran into the room at full speed, skidding to a stop to be inundated with hugs and shouts of joy. The family crowded together, linked to each other in one or multiple ways.

Sylvie stood from her chair and approached the group. She placed a hand on Roni's back and her friend turned to receive a hug. Sylvie released her to offer a hand to Wade.

"Congratulations, Dad," she said. Wade responded by pushing away her extended hand and pulling her up into a tight bear hug, lifting the tiny chief off the ground.

Ian pushed up in his chair at the sight, not liking it one bit. The words *get your hands off her* sprang to the tip of his tongue. The absurdity of thinking such a thing kept his lips sealed. Sylvie didn't belong to anyone and she wanted to keep it that way.

"Is he really my brother?" Wade asked. It was the first time the man had referenced Ian since the moment Michael had announced his identity. The car ride over he'd been focused on Lacey.

"That he is," Michael replied. "I wouldn't have told him otherwise."

"How did you find him?"

Ian wanted to know the answer to that question, too.

"When Luke was a baby he suffered two cracks in his inner clavicle. He fell off his changing table and displaced the bones. Plates were put in to realign the collarbone, but it was such a unique break I knew I just needed to search hospital records for someone with plates in their right shoulder. I've been looking for years. Then two weeks ago I was notified we found a match. An Ian Stone from Pasadena, California, entered a hospital for surgery on his shoulder. His X-rays showed evidence of the exact same break as Luke Spencer's. The plates were still intact. Although I'm not sure how, since there was evidence they underwent severe pressure. Some sort of altercation, I presume, but at any rate, I visited Luke in the hospital when he woke up. He was forthcoming in offering a blood test." Michael waved a hand at Ian. "There's no scientific doubt that this is Luke Spencer."

"He may be Luke Spencer, but that doesn't make him our brother," Roni spoke, her hard gaze locked on Ian's.

Ian caught Sylvie's frown at her friend's words, but he kept his expression blasé. Roni was right. He didn't fit in as a family member with these people, but he only needed his blood to claim his inheritance and start his life as a business owner. He could finally be a man to be respected.

"Just tell me what my take is and I'll be on my way."

"What is that supposed to mean?" Wade asked.

"Simple. You two have had your shares your whole life, while I've lived in poverty. Now it's my turn."

Wade scoffed. "Not so fast. I have questions that need to be answered first."

"Ask away. My life is an open book."

"Who are your parents?"

"Phil and Cecelia Stone."

Wade looked at Michael. His mouth dropped, and at his grandfather's nod, he closed it on a flare of obvious anger. "Stone. I knew I recognized the name. Phil Stone was our property caretaker when we were young. Before the car crash. Why would our old caretaker kidnap you?"

"I can't answer that one. They're both dead now, their secrets taken to the grave with them. Maybe our grandfather knows." Ian looked to Michael. "He seems to know more than anyone."

Michael shook his head, his hands opened palm up, empty.

"I know." Clay Spencer interrupted the exchange. His chin quivered before he blew out a breath.

The room fell to bated-breath silence.

"The Stones quit right away. Right after the accident, Phil came to me and said he and his wife couldn't take the aftermath of the accident and the injured kids. It was too much for them. I didn't fault them because it was too much for everyone. No one knew how to react."

"Uncle Clay, that doesn't tell us why the Stones took Luke," Wade pointed out.

Clay bobbed his head, his skin beaded with sweat. His breath grew erratic. "I overheard a telephone conversation between Meredith and Michael. After that I made a call to my friend and relayed it."

"Your friend. The one who killed our parents?" Wade asked.

Clay frowned, his shoulders slumped with a nod. He looked at Ian and said, "You have to understand why I trusted him. My friend told me my brother had married a Russian spy. I believed him. I was wrong to. I'm sorry, Luke."

Luke?

The name threw him. It didn't feel right. But before he could correct the uncle, Clay continued with what he knew of that horrifying day.

"Phil Stone had been in the house when I made the call to my friend. I didn't know Phil overheard me, but he must have. I told my friend they had taken a bag of gold and weren't coming back. I told him where it was hidden. Phil heard it all."

"I'm still not following. Why did he take Luke?" Wade's voice rose.

"Because Luke was the golden child," Michael answered for Clay. "Now I understand."

Ian scoffed. The title rubbed him in a degrading way, even more than being called Luke. It was a smack in the face when he wasn't worth two pennies. "Sorry, Gramps," he said. "I am not a golden child."

Clay looked him dead-on. "I'm surprised you're alive. Once Phil had what he wanted, he could have left you for dead."

"And just what did he want?"

"The gold," Michael responded. "I told Meredith to pack her family up and run. In my line of work, I have a lot of enemies, and one of them had found her. Clay's friend used him to get information on her and told my enemies where she was. They would kill her to get to me. Her mountain was no longer safe, so I told her they would never be returning to Norcastle. She had a bag of gold and jewels for such an occasion. It's the way of things when one works in the CIA. Or has family in it. I told her to hide the bag of gold on the baby. In Luke's diaper to be exact." Michael looked at Ian. "*Your* diaper."

"Ew," Roni said to no one.

Michael continued, "It was the one place my enemies wouldn't think to look. Honestly, through the years, I had always thought they figured it out and killed you somewhere else. I never understood why they wouldn't boast about it, though. Regardless of who took you from the scene of the crime, you were taken because you were the golden child. Literally."

"Well, it explains why my father always had money when he didn't work."

"Do you have any idea why Stone kept you?"

Ian knew it wasn't Phil Stone who'd kept him. "My mother couldn't have children. She was always very ill. She always told me I was the only one she could have. She went to her grave with her husband's secret. Maybe she knew it was dangerous to return, because someone has been trying to kill me since the moment I stepped foot into this town."

Ian eyed his family, each individually. Roni, who had given him flak from day one. Michael, who'd notified him, but could have come to regret his choice when he realized Ian only wanted his share of the money. Wade, who looked at Ian with anger. Clay, who knew the Spencers' killer and had relayed a message to him that got Ian stolen from the car in the first place. How much more was the man withholding?

"You shouldn't be surprised that I don't trust any of you," Ian said.

"I wouldn't kill you," Roni spouted. "I've spent every day since I learned you were alive out there looking for you."

Michael chuckled.

"What are you laughing at?" Ian asked. "You're in the CIA. You have ample ways to kill me."

"Son, if I wanted you dead, you'd already be dead."

Ian sighed in frustration, knowing truth when he heard it. He looked to Clay. The uncle raised his hands in surrender. "All I've ever wanted is to give you kids the best life I could. For my brother. He was my best friend. I owed him that and more. No, I am not trying to kill you. I rejoice that you're home, finally, where you belong."

Sylvie's cell phone rang. She turned around to take the call, saying, "Hello, Mrs. Cole. How's Jaxon doing?" as she moved away for privacy.

Ian said to Wade, "Well? That leaves you, big brother. You haven't said much, but that could be a cover-up, pretending to know nothing when you actually do. I bet you feel all protective of the family. Like you can't let anyone near them who might take advantage."

"That would be true."

"So, knowing I only want my share and couldn't care less about the rest of you must really irk you."

"Also true." Wade's jaw ticked.

"Ian." Sylvie had returned and now spoke behind him. He waved a hand as he attempted to get to the bottom of this with his brother.

"So you thought you could get rid of me before I made waves for everyone."

"Ian," she spoke again, a desperate tone in her voice.

He turned and was faced with stark-white fear. He reached for her and she let him take her in his arms. He grabbed her face to force her to look at him. "Tell me. What's wrong?"

"It's Jaxon. Mrs. Cole went to go check on him in the spare bedroom and he wasn't there. She can't find him anywhere. I have to go look for him."

"Let's go." Ian placed an arm on the back of her vest and nudged her forward.

"No." Sylvie dug in her heels. "I can't protect you while I search." To Michael, she said, "I don't believe for a second any of you are trying to kill Ian, but the truth is someone is. I've witnessed the attempts myself, so before I leave I need to know he'll be kept safe."

"Sylvie, I can take care of myself," Ian said. She placed a hand up to stop him. "I'm coming with you."

"Not to worry, Chief," Michael assured. "I've got my men all over this place now. No one will get near him."

"Your men are here now?" Sylvie asked.

"I don't go anywhere without them."

Sylvie looked around the room at the few people in chairs.

"If they could be seen, they wouldn't be working for me anymore."

"Right…" She cleared her throat. "Okay then, Ian, I think you're in good hands." She reached for his face and placed her left hand on his cheek. "Open your eyes. Don't be afraid to let them in." She whispered the last part as she leaned in to kiss his cheek.

The kiss felt final, like a goodbye.

No way.

Before Ian gave it a second thought, he maneuvered his face to meet her lips with his.

Her soft lips hardened beneath his purposeful ones. If Sylvie thought this was a farewell, she had another think coming.

Ian pressed in, pulling her forearms toward him. She didn't push away, but she also didn't kiss him back. He didn't care. Let her remember the feel of him. Let her second-guess her self-denial of a companion in life. So what if she'd had two tries blow up in her face?

As amazing as she felt in his arms, he knew she needed to find her son. Ian released her lips and arms and leaned away from her. She didn't move forward or back, stunned with a petrified look in her dilating eyes. Not the look he'd hoped for, but it would do. Sometimes fear got a person to make a move.

"Don't be afraid, Sylvie." He used her same words to make his point.

She snapped to attention. A look in the direction of his family flushed her cheeks. The tough and mighty chief of police was blushing.

And she was absolutely adorable.

Ian kept that to himself. He'd already sideswiped her once tonight. He'd save more of that for later.

And there would be a later.

She touched her fingertips to her lips. "I'll call you when I've found Jaxon. He couldn't have gone far.

Thank you, Michael, for helping me. This doesn't mean I'm stopping my investigation into the shooter. My team is still on it, and I'll be back ASAP. Congratulations again, Wade. Give Lacey my love."

Sylvie turned tail and beelined it for the exit, a mother on a mission to find her son, even if she was a bit flustered doing it. Less than a minute later her cruiser's lights flashed red and blue as it sped out of the parking lot.

Now Ian found himself in the last place he wanted to be.

"Anyone up for a game of Go Fish?" he asked half-heartedly.

"Yeah," Roni answered. "Go fishing for your cut somewhere else."

"Enough," Wade said. "This is supposed to be one of the happiest moments of my life. I don't want any words said out of pain or anger to mess it up."

Roni let her hands fall to her side. "You're right. I'm sorry. Do you have a name yet for the little guy?"

Wade looked at Ian across the group.

"Oh, man, don't even tell me," Ian scoffed.

"Yeah, we had decided to name him after you. Luke Spencer."

Ian lifted his hands. "It's just as well. As much as you said you wanted me back home, you were really looking for a baby. The adult Luke will only prove a huge disappointment."

NINE

"Dispatch to Chief." Sylvie's radio chirped at her ear.

"Chief here. Go ahead, Carla."

"What's this story I hear?"

Sylvie rolled her eyes and touched her lips again. How fast news spread around here. The minty taste of Ian's lips hadn't even worn off yet. The press of his lips still tingled.

"It was just a kiss. It meant nothing. The man was showing off in front of his family. That's all."

"Whoa. Are you telling me someone kissed you, Chief? Now *that's* a story I do want to hear."

Sylvie groaned at her slip. That wasn't the tale Carla had been referencing. "Oh, you mean about Jaxon. He probably just went for a walk. I have an idea where he is. If I need help, I'll radio in."

"He's a teenager. They're flighty. I'm sure there's nothing to worry about. He's safe. No one would hurt the chief's son." Carla cackled.

"It's not hurting him that I'm worried about." Sylvie thought of Greg. Her son had to be with him. It was the only logical explanation for him leaving without permission. He wouldn't realize Greg wasn't here for Jaxon's benefit, but for his alone. Greg would say all the right things to the boy and trick him into trusting him. Sylvie knew all his moves. She'd fallen for them once. A poor choice.

But then, there was always somebody who would find fault with any decision she'd ever made.

She's keeping the baby? How will she support it?

She's going to school? Who will raise the child?

She wants to be a cop? What if she dies and leaves the child an orphan?

She shook her head. *It's called life, people, and one makes the best decisions they can with what resources they have at the moment.* And up until this moment, what she'd done had worked.

So what changed? The answer wouldn't come until she found her son, but she knew it stemmed from more than Greg's return. The distance with her son had been growing for a couple months.

Her radio chirped in. "Chief, Preston here. You need help? And don't tell me to hold down the fort this time."

Sylvie smiled at her right-hand man's comment. She took the next left into downtown Norcastle. "I think I know where he is. I'm heading there now."

"Is Stone joining you?"

"No, I was able to arrange security detail for him. We need to catch the perp after him, though. I don't like having this lunatic out there on the loose. At least Stone is his only target. But have Smitty and Karl stick close to Stone in case the guy makes another move. He's at the hospital with the Spencers right now. Lacey Spencer had her baby."

"That's got to be uncomfortable for Stone, hanging with a strange family during a birth."

Preston didn't know the half of it. "That's why I need to retrieve my son and get back there."

A car up ahead was pulled off to the side of the road with its hood up. Sylvie slowed her car. "Preston, I've got a disabled vehicle on the south end of Chester Hill Road. I'll stop to let them know someone is on the way to assist them. I can't give them any more time than that. You got this?"

"You can count on me, Chief."

She signed off and slowed her cruiser as she approached the car. Her wheels crunched over hard snow as she brought her vehicle up behind it.

A pop followed by her steering wheel jerking to the right surprised her. Sylvie gripped her wheel through what could only be a blowout. The timing for a flat couldn't have been worse.

Before she could form a decision on her next move, a small Legends racing car came barreling down the embankment, aiming straight for her door.

Not a blowout, she realized.

A setup.

Ian's shooter must think he was still with her, and this was another attempt to get him.

Sylvie shot her body over to the passenger seat for the expectant impact. She shielded her head from any glass bound to come her way, but instead of crashing into her, the car spun out alongside the cruiser, door to door.

Sylvie lifted her head, but in the darkness couldn't make out the driver. He drove off down the road before she could get a better look.

She put her car into gear, but with a thumping driver's side tire she wouldn't get far. Soon, sparks flew up from her front end, and the car hobbled as it rode on its rim, the tire shredded.

The end of the road.

The Legends car had no taillights, race cars didn't

need them, and that meant the driver had disappeared into the night. The perfect getaway car, even with the small motorcycle engine. With her wheel shot, she wasn't going anywhere. The one thing she'd learned from this incident was that their killer had access to the race track. Since most of the town worked at the track in some way, that left only 10 percent of the town in the clear.

She hit her radio. "Preston. The disabled vehicle was a trap. I was ambushed, my tire blown out. I've lost him at this point." She hit her steering wheel at being bested. "The guy pulled up alongside of me, probably looking for Ian. When he saw I was alone, he took off."

Preston chirped in, "Be there in three."

Sylvie veered her car over to the side of the desolate back road and parked it. A minute passed, then two. Three came with still no sign of Preston. She opened her door and got out to inspect her tire…or the burned rubber that was left.

She straightened and went to retrieve the jack and spare tire. She'd have to have a talk with Preston on his response time. It was going on five minutes.

She lifted the trunk on a creak and fumbled in the dark. The sound of the snowy wilderness around her hummed with a gusty wind whipping through the branches and swaying the leafless treetops. She had the car jacked up in record time. As she cranked the lug nuts off and looked down the road behind her, she hit her radio, getting more irritated by the second.

"Preston, where are you?" She reached for the tire and replaced the disintegrated one with the small doughnut. She wouldn't be chasing any bad guys on it, but she'd get to Jaxon all right.

No response came on her radio.

She gave a last twist of her wrench and stood. Dusting the snow from her pants, she keyed her radio again.

"Never mind, Preston, I got it. Thanks, but no thanks. I want you in my office come morning. I don't care if it's Christmas Eve."

She switched frequencies to the rest of her men. "Dispatcher."

"Here, Chief."

"I need a tow truck out on Chester Hill. There's a car I need an owner ID on. Not that I'm expecting it to be legit. The thing's probably stolen."

"You got it."

Sylvie threw the tools into the trunk of her cruiser, but before she shut the lid, a crunching sound came from behind her.

She had her gun drawn and was about to turn when a hard force hit the back of her head. Pain radiated through her whole body in shock waves as her knees gave out.

A groan escaped from her lips. Her body began to fall, but someone caught her up under her arms.

The world of trees and snow tilted and swirled around her. She fought to keep conscious, but darkness fought back with a vengeance.

She tried to focus on who had her, but her mind didn't function as it should. The blunt trauma to her head demanded its time to register throughout her nervous system.

She hit cold metal, and it took her a second to realize she was in her trunk, her face plastered against the tools she'd just used to change the tire.

Her body jolted when the trunk's lid slammed down in place. The car's engine roared to life. She was being

FREE Merchandise is 'in the Cards' for you!

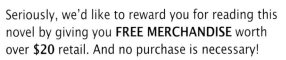

Dear Reader,

We're giving away FREE MERCHANDISE!

Seriously, we'd like to reward you for reading this novel by giving you **FREE MERCHANDISE** worth over $20 retail. And no purchase is necessary!

You see the Jack of Hearts sticker above? Paste that sticker in the box on the Free Merchandise Voucher inside. Return the Voucher today... and we'll send you Free Merchandise!

Thanks again for reading one of our novels—and enjoy your Free Merchandise with our compliments!

Pam Powers

Pam Powers

P.S. Look inside to see what Free Merchandise is **"in the cards"** for you!

We'd like to send you two free books like the one you are enjoying now. Your two books have a combined price of over $10 retail, but they are yours to keep absolutely FREE! We'll even send you 2 wonderful surprise gifts. You can't lose!

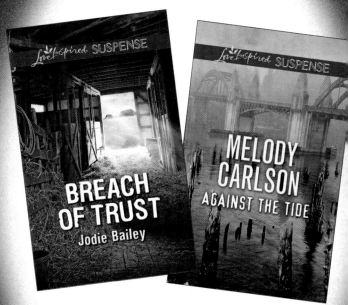

REMEMBER: Your Free Merchandise, consisting of **2 Free Books** and **2 Free Gifts**, is worth over $20 retail! No purchase is necessary, so please send for your Free Merchandise today.

Get TWO FREE GIFTS!

We'll also send you 2 wonderful FREE GIFTS (worth about $10 retail), in addition to your 2 Free books!

Visit us at:
www.ReaderService.com

▶ Detach card and mail today. No stamp needed.

FREE MERCHANDISE VOUCHER

2 FREE
BOOKS
and
2 FREE
GIFTS

Please send my Free Merchandise, consisting of
2 Free Books and **2 Free Mystery Gifts**.
I understand that I am under no obligation to buy
anything, as explained on the back of this card.

❏ I prefer the regular-print edition   ❏ I prefer the larger-print edition
153/353 IDL GLJS   107/307 IDL GLJS

Please Print

FIRST NAME

LAST NAME

ADDRESS

APT.#   CITY

STATE/PROV.   ZIP/POSTAL CODE

Offer limited to one per household and not applicable to series that subscriber is currently receiving.
Your Privacy—The Reader Service is committed to protecting your privacy. Our Privacy Policy is available
online at www.ReaderService.com or upon request from the Reader Service. We make a portion of our mailing
list available to reputable third parties that offer products we believe may interest you. If you prefer that we not
exchange your name with third parties, or if you wish to clarify or modify your communication preferences, please
visit us at www.ReaderService.com/consumerschoice or write to us at Reader Service Preference Service, P.O. Box
9062, Buffalo, NY 14240-9062. Include your complete name and address.

NO PURCHASE NECESSARY!

SLI-N16-FMC15

◄ If offer card is missing write to: Reader Service, P.O. Box 1867, Buffalo, NY 14240-1867 or visit www.ReaderService.com ◄

BUSINESS REPLY MAIL

FIRST-CLASS MAIL   PERMIT NO. 717   BUFFALO, NY

POSTAGE WILL BE PAID BY ADDRESSEE

READER SERVICE
PO BOX 1867
BUFFALO NY 14240-9952

NO POSTAGE
NECESSARY
IF MAILED
IN THE
UNITED STATES

moved to places unknown, and she couldn't lift a hand to stop it.

As the darkness of her mind won the battle over consciousness, her last image was of Ian smiling down at her son.

Roni ended a call on her cell phone. "Listen up, everyone. Spencer Speedway has trouble. Criminal trouble. I just took a call from our head mechanic. He called to tell me Brett Dolan's Legends car is missing. Someone's stolen it. He also said he's pretty sure someone cut the brake lines to the number eleven car. That accident on the track at the Jingle Bell Jam was no accident. It was sabotage."

"Aren't the Legends cars the ones Jaxon was driving?" Ian asked.

Roni looked at Ian like he'd sprouted a second head. "Didn't you hear me? The brake lines were cut on number eleven."

"So?"

"So, number eleven *is* Jaxon's car. Someone cut Jaxon's lines. He could have died in that wreck." He saw Roni shiver and reach for her neck. She pulled up her collar over the burn scars. Ian wondered how much she remembered from her crash, but something else raising the hairs on the back of his neck took a front seat.

"Someone tried to hurt the chief's son?" he said, while his mind computed the details. "At the same moment someone took a shot at me."

"Are you sure it was at *you*?" Michael asked from his waiting-room chair. He stood and raised a handheld device. "Because my men have been looking for hours for someone trailing you or staking claim to finding you, and they don't have any leads. From what they can tell, no one's after you like you believe. Besides, Jaxon's brakes would have been tampered with before you arrived at the race. My gut's telling me the shots have been meant for Sylvie, not you."

"Sylvie? This whole time? The gunshots at the track as well as on the highway? The car explosion she…she nearly died in. The snowmobile tracks she would have followed off the mountain's edge to her…death. Even the shot at the department… It was all aimed at *her*?"

Ian looked to the hospital's exit, then remembered she'd sped off to find Jaxon.

"Why did that boy have to run off tonight?" he said in frustration.

Michael cleared his throat, but Ian was already on it.

"He didn't run off," Ian said.

"You're a smart man." Michael got on his device and started issuing orders to track down Sylvie. She was heading straight into another trap. And this time alone.

TEN

"Her cell still goes right to voice mail," Ian said as he handed Roni back her phone for the tenth time. "Sylvie might be in a place with no coverage." He hoped that was the case. "How familiar are you with Jaxon's birth father, Greg?"

Roni looked at Ian from the backseat. "He grew up here. Why? Did Sylvie tell you about him?"

"I met him."

"You met Greg? How? When?"

"The man's back in town. He wants custody of Jaxon. Says Sylvie's unfit. You and I both know that's not true."

"Greg's in Norcastle?"

"He was as of this morning. If he's got Jaxon, who knows where they are by now."

"Kidnapping wouldn't get him custody," Roni said.

"True, but feeding lies to the boy to get him to run away wouldn't be kidnapping. He would be able to use it as evidence of Sylvie's lack of parenting skills."

"Right." Roni pressed her lips. "Sylvie's going to need some money. She won't be able to fight him on her salary. I'll make sure she has it."

"Thank you." Ian felt a pang of disappointment,

wanting to be the one to help her, but what did it matter where the money came from as long as she had it?

Roni eyed him and he knew she was speculating.

"She's a friend, okay?" he said. "I know we just met this week, but she's the most genuine person I've ever known."

Roni nodded. "I guess we do agree on something... Ian."

She dropped her gaze to her lap. He knew she wanted to call him Luke, but something held her back. Something he saw, too.

He wasn't the Luke Spencer everyone wanted.

"I think we can also agree on the tasks ahead of us. Find Jaxon and Sylvie. Can we do that?" he asked.

She nodded and looked him in the eyes. Her ice blues matched his own, and for the first time he saw the resemblance. But eye color didn't make them family.

Michael pulled the SUV up to the police station. The four of them jumped out and barged in on Carla talking on the phone.

She took one look at their faces and said to the person on the line, "I gotta go. Something's come up." She dropped the phone on its cradle and turned to them. "Why do I get the feeling my shift's not over?"

"Have you heard from Sylvie?" Ian asked.

"Sure." Carla smiled up at Ian in a weird way. "Don't give up on her. She's bound to see you're worth breaking her life of singlehood."

Ian had no idea what the woman was going on about. "Just tell me when you talked to her."

"Humph." The woman moved her mouse to wake the screen up. "Perhaps you don't understand. I'm on your side, son. You could be really good for our chief."

"Your chief is good all on her own. Perhaps *you* shouldn't be giving up on her."

Carla paused her search on her screen, effectively chastened. "Of course, I just heard someone kissed her and thought—"

"Well, don't think. Just tell me when you spoke to her, and then I'll need you to radio her again."

Carla read from the screen. "Her call came in about an hour ago at 10:33 tonight. What's this about?" she asked as she reached for her microphone. "Dispatch to Chief."

Carla unclicked the microphone's lever and waited for Ian's answer while she waited for Sylvie to respond.

"Jaxon ran off and Sylvie went after him."

"I know that. That's what you're all upset about? They didn't give her the job for no reason. She knows what she's doing. She'll find her son, and if she needs help she'll call it in."

Carla clicked the microphone again. "Dispatch to Chief. Do you read?"

"We think it might have been a setup. We think the shooter has actually been after *her.* I've been in the way, indirectly foiling their attempts."

Carla's face washed white with red blotches. "Oh, no," she uttered. She looked at the screen. "I have access to all the channels assigned to the department, and I heard Sylvie radio Preston to tell him she was pulling over to help a disabled vehicle. It was most definitely a setup. She said someone in one of the Legends cars pulled up alongside her and drove off when they realized you weren't with her. She said they blew out her tire so she couldn't go after them. She had to change the flat. She radioed in to say she was all set and good to go. That was the last I heard from her." Carla pressed the lever. "Chief, I need a response, now."

Silence filled the station and one of the officers in the back of the bull pen came forward.

"What's going on?" he asked. Ian recognized him as Smitty.

"Sylvie's not responding. She ran into some trouble before, but checked back with me to say all was well. But now, something doesn't feel right."

"Where was her last location?" Officer Smitty asked.

"South end of Chester Hill. She was heading to find Jaxon. She thought he would be down there."

Officer Smitty made his way to the door. "I'll take care of this." He rushed out into the night.

Carla looked up. "Now what, Mr. Stone?"

"Spencer," Roni interrupted. "His name is Mr. Luke Spencer."

Carla's eyes grew wide with slow understanding. She sputtered, "Y-you're Luke Spencer?"

"I was," Ian confirmed.

"No wonder the chief wouldn't let you out of her sight. I thought maybe she, well, never mind. I was wrong. You were her responsibility, is all."

"Right, that's all," Ian said, ignoring the iron weight in his gut her words produced. Even if they were true. "Where does that road lead?" Ian asked, attempting to get back to finding Sylvie.

"To the boat landing for entry into the river. That's about it. That, and the back way into Evergreen."

"Evergreen. The campground?"

"That's right. You were there this morning, so you should know the place is pretty secluded. Not much out there but some trails, icy water and an old covered bridge."

"The covered bridge," Ian repeated, a memory clicking into place. "That's got to be it. She told me Jaxon liked to hike to it from their home. That must be where she was heading. I need a car."

"I'll take you," Michael said. "Roni and Clay, head back, but be ready for direction if we need you."

Carla opened her drawer and handed over a handheld radio. "In case she radios in, you'll hear her." Carla tossed the radio into Ian's waiting hand.

They moved for the door and out into the blustery evening, where snow whipped their faces with shards of ice.

Ian pulled up the collar of the police winter coat he still wore. He leaned into the wind and pressed toward Michael's SUV. "It's getting worse!" he shouted from over the hood of the truck, both jumping into the front seats, slamming the doors on the loud roar of wind.

"Do you remember the way?" Michael asked.

Ian gave out the directions while Michael sent a voice message to his men. "Fall in," he said.

Ian looked in his passenger-side mirror, wondering where the men were. He caught a glimpse of movement followed by car lights flickering on one by one.

"Eight cars? Do you always travel with this much heat?"

"I'm the former director of the CIA. Have I told you I have a lot of enemies?"

"You mentioned it, but how do I know you're not taking me to my demise? I'm still not totally convinced you invited me back here for a heartwarming family reunion."

Michael eyed him. He reached inside his coat pocket and removed a gun. The butt fit snuggly in his palm, his finger hovered over the trigger.

Ian's throat closed at the weapon, ready to fire. Would the guy off him right here in the front seat?

"Why so nervous?" Michael said with a laugh. "I checked you out and know you have a gun permit."

"So?"

"So I'm giving it to you." With that, the man passed the gun over to Ian. The metal felt warm from being close to the man.

"Why?"

"So you'll trust me. I mean you no harm. Finding you has been my life's mission. Bringing my Meredith's family back together for her has consumed me. She died because of this life I live. I couldn't die until I made it right. Keep the gun on me for however long you need to."

"What about your men? Won't they shoot me if they see I'm holding a gun on you?"

Michael spoke into his device to inform his men to ignore Ian's gun. Some laughs came back with a 10-4.

"Why did they laugh?"

Michael shrugged. "You have to understand, we're the closest thing to family each of us has. We keep a distance from our real families to protect them. Most of them are single for life. I'm a father to them, and they are my sons. But when they first come on board we have a time of earning each other's trust. I hand them my weapon until they know they can trust me. It always ends the same."

"How's that? Take the next right," Ian instructed.

"I give them my trust, and soon, they find themselves guarding me with their lives."

"And you think I'll do the same?"

"Just wait," Michael replied and pulled into the Evergreen Haven Campground.

They plowed through the new snow on the ground while more falling snow blinded the area to them.

"The covered bridge is up this road after you pass the big cabin."

Ian looked at the dark structure as they passed by. Yellow police tape blocked the door, leftover from the crime committed that morning.

Michael pulled the SUV up to the bridge and put the vehicle in Park. "End of the road, I'd say. This bridge was built for horse and buggies, not big military SUVs."

"Leave your headlights on. I'll go in and search inside."

Michael put a hand on Ian's arm to stop him. "I can have my men search it. I didn't bring you back here to die."

"You didn't bring me back here. I came for my own reasons."

"The money."

"To be worth something, and that means I go out there and find Sylvie."

Ian jumped out into the storm and pressed against its power. The wind mixed with the roaring water of the river below. He peered over the edge as he forged through the snowdrifts up to the covered bridge.

The headlights of the SUV and arriving cars cast light inside, but still there were shadows on the edges.

"Jaxon! Sylvie!" he yelled and tried to hear through the storm hitting the roof.

Nothing at first, but then a whimper off to his left pulled him around.

Ian followed the sound. "Jaxon? Is that you?"

His foot tripped on something. He dropped to the floor and touched a leg. A boot.

"Jaxon, it's just me, Ian." Ian's heart rate picked up. To the men outside, he hollered, "I found him!"

Jaxon shook with a viciousness of hypothermia setting in. Michael and his men bounded inside the old wooden structure, their boots thudding on the planks. They appeared around Ian to assist in moving the boy.

Jaxon let out a wail.

"Is it your leg?" Ian froze in lifting him.

He barreled his head into Ian's neck, but no response came. The boy was being as brave as possible. Ian wouldn't make him stay out here longer than necessary. He trudged through the snow to the SUV. Michael held the back door open wide. When Ian placed Jaxon on the seat beside him, the teen gripped stiff arms around him and cried aloud. Ian knew this wasn't about a pained leg. This was a cry of guilt.

"It's okay, Jaxon. No one is angry. Worried, yes, but not angry. Can you tell me what happened?" Jaxon shook, his teeth chattering while the heat roared around them.

Michael opened the front door and peered in. "She's nowhere around here."

Ian saw the influx of CIA agents perusing the bridge inside and below, down on the riverbanks, flashlight beams bouncing in every direction through the snow. Ian's heart sank.

"So she never made it." He sighed in frustration. "Michael, hand me the police radio." Once it was in his hand, Ian hit the button to speak. "In case you're listening, Sylvie, your son is safe. Hang on, sweetheart, we're coming for you next."

ELEVEN

Sylvie's eyes shot open on a sharp inhale. Pain struck her senses, and she reached for her head. She groaned as she touched dried blood in her loose ponytail.

How long had she been out? Hours? Days?

She licked parched lips and surveyed her surroundings.

Darkness ensconced her, but somewhere off in the distance a slip of light beckoned. Less than a crack, a sliver, but it had to open to so much more.

If she could reach it.

Sylvie pushed up on weakened hands. No binds of any kind hindered her. At her waist, she found her belt and gun gone. At her shoulder, her radio torn from its place.

She crawled a few feet toward the light and found dirt and old leaves beneath her. She lifted her chin to feel a breeze stir through the dank room. The outside was behind that crack.

She pushed to her feet, her hands on her knees until the dizzying pain subsided a bit. Her first steps slogged. At the crack, she pried her fingers inside and stood on tiptoes to see through to the other side.

Her eyes flinched at the sunlight's glare. Pristine,

newly fallen snow blinded her. She squinted off to the right to allow her eyes to adjust. A black pipe came into view. No, too thick to be a pipe.

A smokestack.

Instantly, Sylvie knew her location.

She'd been dumped inside one of the vacant mills down by the river.

Knowing her location motivated her to use all her might to pull, push and break the wood to get to the other side.

Not a splinter budged from its place.

More elbow jabs and even a good high sidekick that sent her slamming back to the cement only jarred her teeth and nothing more.

She needed to find another way out.

She gave the board one more halfhearted kick before heading back into the darkness.

Careful steps led to a wall, a guide she used to feel her way from corner to corner. For all she knew she could be retracing her steps. At a point where the wall turned another corner, another crack of light gave her a destination. As she neared it a voice filtered to her ears.

Someone was nearby.

Her kidnapper?

She turned an ear to the sound and closed in. A conversation between two men drifted to her. One laughed and said, "We hit the jackpot with this one."

Sylvie paused. Were they talking about her? It couldn't be. She wasn't worth much. If they thought her family would pay out, they'd picked the wrong person.

She softly stepped up to the crack and found it to be a door. Without her gun she couldn't burst in. A fool's move if there ever was one.

The other man spoke. "How much longer before you're in the Spencer accounts?"

Sylvie froze. Her breath crystallized in her lungs. Was she hearing right? Were these guys hackers?

She stepped back. Her foot chinked against a piece of wood, sending it over in an echoing topple.

"Shh…someone's here. Check it out. I got you covered." A chair scraped along the floor. A gun clicked.

Sylvie backed away against the dark wall. She picked up her steps and found another corner to hide behind just as the door opened wide, pouring light over the place she'd stood moments before.

A flashlight beam roamed across the floor by her feet. Just an inch more and the tips of her shoes would be seen.

Sylvie held her breath and her body in check. More than anything she wanted to know who the men were, but their weapon gave them the upper hand.

For now.

She knew their hideout. She would be back ASAP with her men.

But that was only if she made it out of here first.

With that being the only door she'd found so far, it might be a while.

"Cops are pulling up," the guy in the other room shouted on a rush.

Sylvie's pulse tripped. Help was here?

"Which cop?" the guy with the flashlight asked.

"Looks like Smitty."

The guy talking didn't seem worried that Smitty was here. What did this mean? Was Smitty involved with these guys?

The thought sickened her. It couldn't be true. Smitty

had been a devoted officer in this town for many years. He was like a father to her. He had helped her so much when she was young and pregnant, and then later getting situated at the department.

But he was also devoted to Reggie.

"What's he doing here?" the man at the door whispered back.

"Shh, just don't move and maybe he'll move on by."

Sylvie took their responses as confirmation Smitty was not a part of their ring. She sighed in gratefulness. But she wasn't about to stay silent.

Sylvie opened her mouth and shouted as loud as possible, "Help!"

Suddenly, the man at the door slammed it shut and a scuffle could be heard happening on the other side.

Sylvie rushed around the corner toward the door, but without the light, she tripped over a beam and fell to the floor with a grunt.

She seethed with scrapes and pushed up on her burning palms to gain her feet. By the time she got the door open, the men were gone.

She ran by the computers and out a second door. More darkness followed, but soon light reached her eyes and led the way.

An exit door finally came into view in the enormous mill. She stomped up the stairs out through the door, straight into Smitty's large, beefy arms.

"Chief!"

"Jaxon!"

"He's safe. Ian found him."

Sylvie sagged against him. "Quick, get the team here."

"What happened?" Smitty asked as he reached for

his radio. "We've been looking for you all night. And Preston."

"Preston's missing?"

"Hasn't been responding since you radioed him last night."

Worry for her friend filled her. Quickly, she relayed what she'd overheard in the mill. "Smitty, they're running some sort of hacking ring here. Breaking into bank accounts. Can you handle it?"

He looked to the vacant building behind her with a nod.

"The setup needs to be confiscated right away for evidence before we lose any of it." She looked out into the snow-covered parking lot, the river roaring behind her. They were on the back side of the building, out of view from downtown. "There were two guys running the ring. They ran off as soon as I shouted. They couldn't have gotten far."

"Did they kidnap you?"

"That's what's weird. They had a gun, but they seemed surprised to have me in the building. I don't think they did. It's almost as if someone wanted me to find them."

"Or someone wanted them to find you snooping around their illegal activity so they would take you out."

Sylvie pondered Smitty's idea as she walked to the corner of the building. Snow tracks led from a side door straight to the river's edge. She followed the footprints and peered into the half-frozen rapids below. Empty. A bend in the river inhibited any further tracking. If this was the way they'd come, they wouldn't last long in the river.

She headed back to her officer.

"I think you need to get checked out, Chief," Smitty said. Sylvie reached for her head and felt the dried blood.

"It looks worse than it is. I can still handle the job."

"You can take time. Reggie's back to help."

Sylvie stopped short in the knee-deep snow. "Y-you called Reggie in?"

"I didn't just call him. I went and personally picked him up. He stepped right up, too." Smitty nodded matter-of-factly. "And has done a fine job running the show all night. It sure is good to have him back."

"Found her. And she's fine." The call came in from Smitty. The whole department, inside and still out searching for Sylvie, cheered through the radio lines.

Ian sat beside Jaxon on Sylvie's office couch, her window now boarded up behind them. He took his first full breath since the night before and squeezed wetness from his eyes. Pinching the bridge of his nose, he prayed. *Thank You, God. Thank You for keeping her safe.*

Then he reached for Jaxon. The boy threw himself into Ian's arms and buried his face into the crook of his neck. Wet tears poured out onto Ian's shirt and Ian pressed in and rubbed the boy's head.

He spoke soothing words as Jaxon released the fear he'd held at bay all night long. The boy, not yet a man, put on a good front for the officers. So stoic like his mother, but all along terrified inside.

Ian let Jaxon be that terrified boy now, even though he wanted to jump from Sylvie's couch and grab the radio to demand where she'd been. What had she been through? Did she need comfort like her son? Would she accept it from him? He had so many questions he wanted to ask while he held her in his arms, but he could do none of that in front of her son. Maybe not even alone. Sylvie marked her boundaries clear.

There was no room for anyone but her son and her job.

Her very dangerous job.

Ian could see how the men she dated found it hard to let the reality of her job go. Sitting here with her son in the aftermath of only one night on duty of many nearly undid him. What would a lifetime be like, knowing she could walk out the door and never return because, like she said, her job was to always go in? Go into the danger. Go after the bad guys. Where would that leave him?

Ian pulled Jaxon tighter long after his tears and hiccups subdued. He needed the boy in this moment as much as Jaxon needed him.

Two men who shared their worry for Chief Sylvie Laurent.

But Ian would return to California soon. Jaxon would forever go through nights like this, always knowing they could end worse.

Sylvie's son grew quiet and his breathing steadied. His body listed in Ian's arms.

A glance down showed Jaxon had fallen asleep.

The poor kid had stayed up through the night, and now his body wanted sleep.

Reginald Porter paraded into Sylvie's office. He took note of her sleeping son, then moved forward without a word to her desk chair, looking mighty comfortable.

But then he had been an officer here for over thirty years. In fact he'd been present at the car crash that killed Ian's parents and got him kidnapped.

Could Reggie help him figure some things out about the crash?

"Do you remember the Spencer car crash?" Ian asked in a deep whisper.

His question stunned the man, but Reggie answered, "I do. I was a rookie at the time. Why do you ask?"

"I'm sure you're aware the baby might still be alive."

Reggie nodded. "I've heard something to that effect. Why do you ask?"

"I'm Luke Spencer. Been tested and everything. It's legit. I was kidnapped from the scene by the Spencers' caretaker, Phil Stone."

Reggie let out a long whistle. "Wow. That's…crazy."

"My thoughts exactly. I was wondering what you could tell me about that day."

"Well, Ian… Ah, Luke?"

"Ian's fine."

"Okay, Ian, I remember government officials busting in to take over, so I can't say I had any knowledge about your kidnapping. In fact, we all believed you to be inside the car."

"But you remember the scene."

"You can never forget something like that. Fire…" Reggie cleared his throat and dropped his gaze to his chest—the very chest that had recently gone under the knife. "I would have to think whenever fire is involved, things couldn't be worse, and not just for the victims, but for first responders, too. There's just nothing anyone can do."

"Meaning you have to let them burn."

Reggie swallowed. "I'm sorry. But I will say I sure am glad to see you weren't in that car after all. Wade got his sister out, but she was on fire and he couldn't get back inside to get you. I don't think he ever forgave himself for that. He was just a kid. Eight years old. He must be so relieved to have you back. But where have you been? You said Phil Stone got you out?"

"And kidnapped me for money."

"Kidnapped? There was more to that scene than the feds let on. I'm sorry to hear that. But at least you're alive." Reggie shrugged. "I saw the scene. You should be dead. I'm surprised you made it down the ravine in the first place. That car flipped repeatedly and…well, I'm sure your siblings can tell you what they endured. You don't need me for that."

"You say that, but I get the feeling you like being needed."

"Doesn't everybody?"

Jaxon stirred and mumbled. Ian lowered his voice. "How's your heart?"

Reggie covered his chest with a light rub. A slow smile spread over his face. "You must mean something to the chief for her to confide in you. I'll trust she had a reason, and just say medical technology is remarkable. My ticker is stronger than it has been in a long time. I gotta tell you, I thought I was done for, but now I'm in the best shape of my life. Lost a ton of weight, too."

"Any plans to return to work?"

Reggie rubbed the tips of his fingers along Sylvie's smooth wood-top desk. "I would be lying if I said I didn't miss the force. It's been my whole adult life. Retirement has its good days, but there's only so many repairs a guy can catch up on. I'm driving the wife mad." Reggie gave a low laugh. "Coming back may save the marriage."

"But what would you come back as?"

"Well, that's something I wanted to talk with Sylvie about. If you don't mind—"

"Talk to me about what?" Sylvie stood in the doorway, catching them both by surprise. Her gaze traveled from Reggie sitting at her desk to Ian holding her sleeping son.

Her lips pursed. "Well, doesn't this look comfy. I see it didn't take you boys long to move right in."

TWELVE

"Those men at the factory did not kidnap me. I got the feeling they didn't even know I was there." Sylvie unlocked a cabinet and took out a spare belt. She buckled herself in and withdrew a gun next. Loaded and holstered, she was back in business again.

"I was dumped there. Now get out of my chair," she commanded Reggie.

Reggie relinquished the seat, but Ian had to wonder if the man's newfound health would pose a problem for Sylvie. Would he try to take over her seat permanently? How would she handle that along with everything else that was about to be thrown at her? She didn't even know about her son's brakes yet.

"Of course they kidnapped you," Reggie said, taking the opposite desk chair. "I really think you need to lie low for a while. Take your son up on the mountain for the holiday. Use my cabin. No one will bother you up there with no access roads. It's secluded and safe. Take the sleds and go. Let me stick around and help you here until we figure out who these guys are."

Ian kept his lips sealed as he observed the conversation between the two officers. Reggie's idea sounded reasonable. Sylvie and Jaxon would be safe.

"You want to help me?" She snatched a pencil from the cup on her desk. She marked off a point on the map with a heavy hand and traced the river to a spot farther down. "You can start looking for these guys here. They jumped in the river and could have made it to this bank. I'm sure they won't be running fast after their frigid swim."

"Crazy fools. But if you don't think they kidnapped you, you just might be a fool, too." Reggie stood to leave.

"Stop right there." Sylvie glared. "I won't be running off to the mountains for a vacation. But since you're so fired up to jump back into work, you can start with this. I want an update on the APB for Lieutenant Preston Wallace. Where you all have looked, every rock you have lifted in search of him and where you plan to look today. I want the laptops from the mill processed for an ID. These men were targeting the Spencers' bank accounts. I want to know how far they got."

Reggie nodded walked to the door.

"And one more thing. If you're planning to come out of retirement, you will not speak to me like that again. Now you may leave."

Reggie exited the room on a short huff.

Ian couldn't hold his tongue any longer. "They were hacking Roni's and Wade's accounts?"

She glared his way. "Yeah, it seems like you're not the only one looking for a cut of their money."

Ian cringed at her verbal strike. "Just my inheritance," he defended quietly. "Nothing more."

"Even if it kills you," she flung back.

"News flash. We figured out last night nobody's actually been out to kill me. I was wrong about that."

"Right, and the bullets flying your way have been blanks."

"No, they were very real, but they weren't flying my way—they were flying yours."

Sylvie shrunk back, confusion silencing her.

"That's right, Chief. This whole time the bad guy has been after you." Ian glanced down at Jaxon's lolling head of silky blond hair. More than anything he wanted to stand and reach for her. To hold her so he knew she was alive and well. Fill his arms with her even if she wouldn't stand for it—knowing she wouldn't stand for it. "Yes, Sylvie, you have been the target. You and Jaxon. His car crash at the track wasn't an accident. Someone cut his brake lines. That happened *before* I came to town. It's never been me."

Sylvie's eyes widened and her skin paled instantly. She grabbed at her stomach and dropped slowly into her chair. No more words or commands spilled from her mouth. Her gaze rested on her son's sleeping face as her green eyes misted up.

"He's fine. He's safe. There's no reason to cry. I'm sorry. I didn't mean to deliver that message so poorly. Aw, come on, Sylvie, please don't cry," Ian begged. Her growing tears pouring forth hurt more than splinters under his fingernails. "You can see he's sleeping peacefully."

"But…but he could have been killed. Who would hurt him like that? *Why?*" she wailed and covered her mouth to stifle the sob.

"Someone who wants to hurt you."

"Me. This whole time, it's been me the shots were for."

"I just kept getting in the way."

Sylvie locked her teary-eyed gaze on him and sobered. "You could have been killed. Oh, Ian, I am so sorry."

"Don't you dare apologize to me."

"How can I not? This should be a joyous Christmas for you. If you hadn't been shot you wouldn't have thought the Spencers were out to keep you from claiming your birthright. It could have been an amazing homecoming for you all. And still you sit here protecting my son for me. As soon as you learned you were safe, you should have gone home with your family. Instead, you went after my son."

"He was easy to find. He was right where you said he likes to go."

"The bridge?"

Ian nodded.

Jaxon stirred again.

Ian glanced down at Jaxon's childlike face. The child still present within the maturing boy showed through in his relaxed slumber.

Ian glanced up to find her watching him with a frown. She didn't come across as a jealous person, but perhaps where her son was concerned things were different.

"I'm not getting comfortable if that's what you're thinking," Ian said quietly.

She snapped to attention and looked back at the map. "Good."

"But I will say it's okay for the boy to have a male figure in his life."

"If you even think I am allowing his deadbeat father back in his life—"

"I didn't say anything about Greg. I just meant there will be things Jaxon will only want to talk with another guy about. It's natural. You must know that."

After a few slow seconds, she nodded. "I feel like I'm losing him. He's been so distant lately."

"You're not losing him. He loves you more than life."

She frowned again and reached into her top drawer. "I found this a couple weeks ago when I was doing his laundry. It's a poem." She unfolded the sheet of torn-out loose-leaf paper. "I didn't even know he wrote poetry." She sat quietly reading the words Ian couldn't see, then leaned across her desk and held it out for Ian to read.

He tilted his head and raised his eyebrows at her. "Even on a good day, Sylvie."

Understanding dawned on her face, and she whipped the paper back. "Oh, I'm sorry. I forgot you can't—"

"Read. It's okay, you can say it. It's nothing I don't already know."

Sylvie stood and came around her desk with the poem. She sat on the soft leather two-seater, fitting snuggly beside her son. She brought the piece of paper over for Ian to see.

"Jaxon has beautiful penmanship," she whispered and pointed a finger to the first word. Slowly, she read each word clearly.

Jaded eyes
Once so bright.
Seen too much
But miss so much
And yet, always watching.

She finished and they sat in silence. "Do you think he's talking about me? Have I failed him in some way?"

"Don't do this to yourself, sweetheart. He's a teen-age boy. He's got a lot of confusion going through his head, and even fear. The world is changing for him. But what is constant in his life is you. He can always count on you, and he knows that."

Sylvie sighed and folded the piece of paper up. She slipped it into her son's pants pocket just as a loud snore broke from Jaxon's nose.

Sylvie covered her mouth to stifle a laugh. Her green eyes danced mischievously from above. Beautiful wasn't enough to describe her.

"I think your son is quite talented with his words and you should be so proud to have such a brilliant child."

Her hand dropped to her lap and gone was the laughter in her eyes. "You're smart, too, Ian. Getting letters mixed up doesn't make you an idiot. You've found ways to gain your knowledge a different way, and you shouldn't take that lightly. We're all different and our differences should be celebrated, not criticized."

"Tell that to my father."

"I can't. He died in a car crash thirty years ago." She looked at him pointedly over Jaxon's mussed hair, daring him to defy her.

Phil Stone was not his father. Never had been.

"So I guess it's no father for me, then."

"There's God."

Ian dropped his head back. "He's the most important Father to have, I know that now. I wish I had known it when I was growing up. Life was hard…and lonely."

"I'm sure Roni and Wade felt the same way."

"But they had each other."

"And would open their hearts and homes to you. Trust me. That's all they've wanted since they learned you might be alive somewhere."

"A family if I want it. Is that what you're saying?"

"Families also come with differences that should be celebrated. There will always be people who criticize,

but in the end you can only do what is best for you. And
only you know, Ian, what that is. Is it the Spencers?"
She shrugged a silent answer. "Is it a business waiting
for you in California?" She frowned at those words, but
quickly pressed her lips to cover it up.

Did Sylvie want him to stay?

The thought of her desiring him in her life felt like
what a gift under the tree might feel like.

Joyful.

Exciting.

Special.

Ian smiled at her over her son's head. Without
thought, his head moved a few inches toward her beautiful petite lips. What a gift it would be to kiss her.

He'd kissed her at the hospital, but that had been a
deliberate move to wake her up. This felt unprovoked.

Natural.

She looked at his lips, so close to hers. With her son
sandwiched in between them, Ian would not be able to
get any closer.

The next move would be hers.

Her chin quivered, and her eyes darkened. He
watched how they misted up again.

"No?" he said, regret threading his one word.

Maybe he was wrong about being special.

"It's not possible. I also have a family to consider."
She broke the connection and looked at her son. "Please
understand."

A tear slipped down her cheek and she swiped it
away.

"I'm disappointed, but I understand." Ian wondered
how the woman could crush him and put him in awe at
the same time. He'd never met anyone like her. To have

her on his arm would be a boost to his morale. A benefit to him—but what would she be getting out of the deal?

Money.

The idea of that being a reason for her to choose him felt all wrong. He was glad she didn't go there. Not that she ever would. Which just raised her even higher in his book.

He moved away and caused Jaxon to jolt awake.

"Mom?" her son said in a rush on finding her beside him. Jaxon launched his lanky arms at his mother and she seemed to melt into him as she welcomed him into her strong ones.

"I'm right here, Jax. I'm okay."

"Mom, what happened?" Jaxon burst into heart-wrenching tears. "Where were you?"

"At one of the vacant mills. Shh, honey, everything's fine now."

"Did you catch the bad guys?"

Sylvie pleaded with Ian over her son's head. She didn't want to tell her son of the danger she'd been in—and still was in. But that would mean keeping things from him. "I'm working on it, but I need you to promise me you won't run off again. It's still not safe."

"Someone's still trying to kill Ian?"

"No. Ian is safe now. Isn't that great?" She forced a smile on her lips.

"That *is* great." Jaxon looked at Ian and beamed. "Hey, you know what I just realized?"

Both Ian and Sylvie shook their heads, staring at each other.

"Today is Christmas Eve," Jaxon said, oblivious to the reality of the situation. Jaxon could be orphaned tomorrow, instead of celebrating the birth of Jesus. "Can Ian spend Christmas with us?"

She sent a startled look Ian's way. "I think Ian has his own family to spend Christmas with."

"In name only, and even that's up for debate," Ian cut in.

"Only by your choice. You should give them a chance before you burn that bridge. Besides, there's something healing about breaking bread with someone. Walls come down as the table grows."

"Then consider me at your table."

Sylvie locked her office door with her sleeping son inside.

When she took this job, she never thought she would have to keep him safe.

She poured herself a cup of coffee and took a second to regroup. With her back to her team, she sipped the lukewarm brew and noticed her hand tremble.

No time for that.

She faced the men and Carla at her desk. "All right, it's time to get to work."

"One step ahead of you," Reggie said from his seat in front of one of the hacker's laptops. "You were right about the Spencers being targeted. These guys were about to hit the big time. They already tapped into their bank accounts."

Sylvie moved to stand beside Ian, where he stood looking over Reggie's shoulder. His body emanated anger like an electrical charge.

"So they planned to take the money and run." Ian sneered and scanned the room. "I need to call them. To warn them. These thieves are still out there. Even if you have their equipment, they could still log in somewhere else and empty the accounts. Roni and Wade need to change their accounts and passwords."

The front entrance opened and Preston walked in holding an ice pack to his head.

"Where have you been?" Sylvie demanded, coming around to meet him.

"Climbing out of a ditch," the officer snarled back. He came around Carla and into the bull pen. He dropped the ice pack to his desk, exposing a purplish welt below his eye. "Someone pushed me off the road and I was knocked unconscious. I'll need a tow truck to get the car out."

"What's wrong with your radio?"

"Dead. Better the radio than me, I say. How much longer are we protecting this guy?" Preston curled a fat lip in Ian's direction. "Until we're all dead because of him?"

"You will do your duty, and that's an order," Sylvie commanded him into begrudging, but silent, submission.

"Except what she's not telling you," Ian inserted, "is she's the real target that someone wants dead."

Preston jerked a gaze in Smitty's direction.

"What are you looking at me for?" Smitty shouted back.

"Because we all know you've never been happy about Sylvie taking the chief position."

"Doesn't mean I would kill her. I uphold the law. I don't break it."

"Enough!" Sylvie shouted. "I know none of you are behind the threat to kill me, but someone *did* cut the brakes in my son's Legends car. That's attempted murder, and I want that person found. Right now I'll need a car to go out to the Spencers'. We're down two cruisers at this point. Smitty, can we take yours?"

"We? Why are you taking Stone there?" Preston asked. "If he's not in danger, send him home."

All eyes went to Sylvie. "About that, Pres. Long story short, the Spencers are his family. Ian is really Luke Spencer. Now if you'll excuse me, I need to inform Roni and Wade about the hackers. That needs to come from me. Police matters need to be handled by the book."

"Right," Smitty responded as he tossed her his keys. "We can't be picky and choosy about what we put on the books, right, Sylvie?"

The room fell to a deathly silence. An uneasy feeling ran up Sylvie's spine. Was he referencing her efforts to help the abused women escape? She didn't keep a file in the office to protect all parties, but she did document evidence on a USB drive that she kept hidden off-site. "Everything gets documented, Smitty. Always."

Ian placed a hand on her forearm, bringing her attention to him. "You ready?" he asked. He was anxious to go, but his touch also offered her support.

She stepped back for Ian to move past her for the exit. "Carla, don't let anyone into my office, and watch over my son. All doors are to stay locked. Preston, get yourself to the hospital."

Sylvie stopped at the front door. "Reggie, since you're hanging around, keep looking for my cruiser, and my gun."

"Will do, Sylvie."

"It's Chief. And don't any of you forget it."

THIRTEEN

"It's astounding that any of you survived," Sylvie said quietly as she drove up the mountain road that led to the Spencer mansion. She slowed the cruiser and nodded to the passenger-side window. "That drop-off. That's the ravine you and your family went over."

Ian's stomach twisted at the sight before him. This was the place his life took a turn, or more like a dive, where a family was torn apart, never to be whole again. "Right here?" he asked. "They were… *We* were pushed over here? I can't imagine…"

Sylvie pulled the car over to the side of the road. The land dropped off mere feet from Ian's passenger window. "Something tells me Roni and Wade would both gladly erase their own bank accounts to go back and erase that horrifying day. There's not enough money in the world to make that ride worth it."

Ian's throat closed. He managed to push out, "The guy who did this. He's in jail?"

"For the rest of his life."

Ian stared out at a danger he unbelievably lived through.

Why?

"I don't know why I was spared. If I was just going

to be kidnapped and treated like garbage, why wouldn't God just let me die? This one event led to a life of torment."

Her hand fell to his on his lap. Instant comfort flooded into him. "Believe me when I tell you, Ian, that Wade and Roni have thought the same thing. With Wade's post-traumatic stress disorder and Roni's burns, they have been tormented their whole lives, too. Perhaps you were spared to help them now. To help each other bring a family back together."

Their gazes stared straight out at the steep drop and the many trees that would have been unrelenting obstacles to the careening car that came their way. "Perhaps this is God's way of taking the evil thing done to you all and making it beautiful."

"He makes all things beautiful in its time." He quoted the Scripture from Ecclesiastes. "I know it in my head, but—"

His hand trembled and he fisted it. "Something Carla said has stuck with me."

He looked down at where they were linked, and then up into her expectant green eyes.

"She said the Spencers are always being attacked." Ian blew out a fast breath and continued. "Sylvie, I haven't been any different than any of the others. Worse, even. I'm their own brother and I'm out for myself like one of the greedy hackers."

"No, you're not like the hackers."

"I saw a way to rise above my circumstances, and I took it."

"First of all, you're not being honest with yourself if you think you only came back here for the inheritance. You came back here for a family, and you know it."

Ian averted his gaze, staring back out at the drop-off.

"Second, you're not a thief. A third of Bobby and Meredith's estate belongs to you. Nobody can negate that. A judge would find in your favor. Your name is in their will as a beneficiary."

"Luke Spencer is in their will."

Sylvie inhaled sharply. "You don't think you can ever be Luke Spencer, do you?"

"I know I can't. I needed the money to say goodbye to Ian the Idiot. But to take the money would make me Luke Spencer, and those are shoes I can't fill. I can never be the golden child."

"They're not looking for a golden child. They're looking for their brother."

"Until they learn he's an illiterate drifter."

"Those are your circumstances. They are not who you are. I've been many things in my life that I could have let define me. Unwanted, irresponsible, pregnant out of wedlock, teen mother, sleep deprived, hungry, lost and lonely. But none of those details make me who I am. And neither do yours."

"How do you rise above them to be something better?"

"Well, first thing, money is not the answer. Wade told you that. Money did nothing for his wounds. He left it all behind, ran away to the army, only to gain more wounds. He took matters into his own hands, but that meant he tore down some bridges along the way."

"Yeah, well, I think I've incinerated mine."

"You're a builder. Rebuild them. Right now. It's not too late."

"I wouldn't even know where to start."

"Back when I was nineteen, pregnant and alone, I started with the bridge that was built for me. The one Jesus built from heaven to my heart. I know you said

Alex brought you to church, but do you understand that Jesus brought you to God? Emmanuel means 'God with us.' And that's exactly what Jesus did when He stepped off His throne in heaven to come to earth on that first Christmas morning. He is the bridge that unites us to our Father in heaven. Jesus looked at us and thought we were worth leaving His throne for. He doesn't see our circumstances. He sees our true identities. Ask Him to help you see Wade and Roni the way He sees them, and I'm sure you won't have any problem reaching out to them."

"But I'm nothing like them. I don't even know who I am."

"That's because your identity was stolen from you. Literally." Sylvie leaned in, inches away. She searched his eyes and reached for his face. "Don't you want to take it back? Don't you want to know who you are? You were robbed of your identity, your whole life wiped away in one swipe."

"Just like what these hackers are doing to people's livelihoods. What they planned to do to my…"

"Siblings. Your brother and sister. You can say it. That's who they are. And whether you think you deserve the name, you are their brother, Luke."

Ian's eyelids dropped closed. His head bent forward to her forehead on a slight shake back and forth.

"Yes, you are Luke Spencer, and right now, I see you, not the details of Ian Stone, but who you are behind it all. Strong, noble, larger than life, helpful, resourceful and, most especially, brilliant."

Ian opened his eyes, but didn't lift his head away. Sylvie's eyes liquefied like sparkling pools on a spring morning. "Are you sure you're not seeing yourself in the reflection of my eyes? Because that's how I see you, among a few more characteristics you didn't mention."

"Like what?" She smiled out of one side of her lips.

"I could tell you, but then I would have to kiss you."

Sadness stole her sweet glimmer. Her hands fell away, but he grabbed hold of them. "We both know that can't happen."

Ian nodded but didn't lift away from her. His breathing picked up, and he was pretty sure hers did also. When she squeezed his hands, digging her fingers into his flesh, he knew she was struggling. All because he put her in this situation.

"I'm sorry," he whispered and turned his lips away. His eyes closed on a rushed sigh. "I want to respect your wishes. I do." Still, he held her hand, rubbing his thumb over her soft skin.

"My wishes. Oh, Luke, if you only knew," she whispered.

Abruptly, Ian lifted his face to see hers. He'd heard what she'd called him, but had it been a slip on her part? Or did she think he could really be a Spencer?

No. She may see Luke in him, but Ian knew otherwise. Wishful thinking didn't change anything.

"We better get to Roni's. Warning them is the least I can do before I head back to California."

Sitting across a glass-top table in the expansive Spencer dining room, Michael changed the accounts and passwords of the Spencer fortune on the laptop in front of him while Roni stared Ian down with her icy eyes so much like his. He expected her to kick him under the table at any minute. "So, you're worried our money will be taken and there will be nothing left for you, so you came to warn us. Is that it?" she asked point-blank.

Ian folded his hands on the glass. "I'm not surprised you would see it that way."

"You haven't given us any reason not to."

Ian mumbled under his breath to Sylvie, "I told you the bridge was gone." To Roni and Michael, he said, "You're right, Roni, I haven't, which is why I also came to tell you I won't be collecting my inheritance."

Michael looked up over the laptop. The reflection of the screen glared in his reading glasses but didn't block the surprise on his face. "I told you when I came to see you at the hospital, the money is yours. Meredith and Bobby left all money and insurance policies to their three children equally. That includes you."

"Honestly, I don't want it because I don't like the person I've become because of it. Just knowing it was mine to claim changed me in a few short weeks. 'O accursed hunger of gold.' Virgil's wisdom come true. Can even drive a person to kidnap a child they don't want. And here I thought money was what I needed if I was going to be something other than Ian the Idiot."

"Ian the Idiot?" Roni scrunched her nose. "Why would you call yourself that?"

Ian shrugged. "The name was commonplace in my house growing up." He dropped his gaze. "I have dyslexia."

Roni scoffed. "That's hardly a reason to call someone an idiot."

Ian squared off to lay it all out on the table. "I can't read."

"So?"

"So, my father deemed that enough reason to call me names."

"Well, that's not your home anymore, so you can stop that."

"I'm homeless." Hey, why not bare all? he figured. "My present address is a trailer on a construction worksite. Or had been anyway. Without the money, I'll probably be out of a job, too."

"Why?" Roni tilted her head, her scars peeking out from under her high-collared sweater. He'd seen them before, the shiny, stretched flesh left by the car fire, but after seeing the ravine that caused that fire and those scars, Ian saw how blind he'd been to Roni's pain. She may not have been taken from her home, but she'd suffered. Ian had been so in tune to her privilege, money, fashion, awards, that he'd missed seeing the person behind it all. He'd missed seeing all she had been through and triumphed over. He missed seeing the person Jesus saw when He looked at her.

Suddenly, Ian wanted to know that person, but why should she give him the time of day? "Well? Why will you be fired?" Roni asked.

"Alex won't fire me, but I'd been offered a part in the business, so that will go away."

"For how much?" she asked, crossing her arms and looking like she was about to do a little wheeling and dealing herself.

"Fifteen percent."

"Fifteen percent for how much?" she clarified.

"A million."

"A million! For fifteen percent?" She leaned forward and tapped the glass with her pointer finger. "You tell him you want fifty for that price. I don't care what fancy locations he's building his homes in, you're worth that. In fact, he'd be getting a deal."

Ian felt his eyebrows spike. The word *protected* filled

his mind. How different of a person he would have been with family to watch out for him. "Well, it doesn't really matter now. I'll be going home empty-handed."

"I thought you said you were homeless."

"I just meant California."

"California is where your heart is, then?" Roni asked, her head tilted to let her long red hair drape over her shoulder.

Ian eyed Sylvie from the corners of his eyes before answering. "Actually, my heart is up for grabs."

"Good, then there's hope you'll find it here in Norcastle." Roni looked to the laptop screen. "Are we safe, Michael?"

Their grandfather turned the screen for all to see. "Your money is safe and secure with the highest protection. You'd have to know someone on the inside to hack these walls. Thank you, Luke, for coming here today to warn us. I'm sorry, Chief, that you had to find out the way you did. I'm glad you're safe now, and your son, as well. Great kid you have there. If you need my help figuring out who cut his brakes, let me know. I'd be happy to offer my men to your service. And to figure out who's after you, as well."

"You know, sir, that's not an option. The CIA is not allowed to work on American soil. I would have to call in the FBI before the CIA. It's critical that I keep things by the books. If the council gets word I have the CIA or FBI running the show in Norcastle's jurisdiction, they might use it as a reason to let me go. I'm still under probation for another two months. It's been a long two years. I can't wait for it to be over."

"Two years seems like a steep amount of time for a probationary period."

"It was the only way they would give me the job."

"And now it's coming to an end. Please don't think I'm trying to step on toes, but I might look into your council members. See if any of them might want you fired before your probation is up. Especially if one of them had been hesitant to hire you in the first place."

"Already on it."

"Any of them not a fan?"

Ian sneered. "The mayor himself."

"Mayor Dolan?" Roni jerked back and kicked.

"Ouch!" Ian hollered, bending over to rub his shin. "What was *that* for?"

"You can't go around defaming people without evidence. Tell him that, Sylvie. That's illegal."

Sylvie remained her stoic self.

"Sylvie?" Roni said slowly. "Is there evidence to support such an accusation against Mayor Dolan?"

Sylvie nodded once then swallowed hard. "Roni, I know this is a shock. Shawn Dolan is somewhat of a star around here. His success on the racetrack has made him a success at the polls, but things aren't always as they seem."

Roni pulled down her collar to reveal her scars more fully. "You don't have to explain appearances to me. You forget I've spent most of my life covering up the truth for the sake of appearances." To Ian she explained, "I used to wear silk scarves to cover my scars up. I told myself it was for everyone else's benefit, but the truth went deeper than that."

Sylvie replied, "I haven't forgotten. That's why I know you'll understand if I have to go against popular opinion someday and arrest Shawn Dolan."

"Arrest him? For what?"

"I'm not at liberty to say. I pray someday the truth is out and all parties are safe." Sylvie pressed her lips together and looked to Ian. He reached out and held her hand on the table.

"I second that," he said. Such a small hand for such a dangerous job. Impending doom hovered over Sylvie, but she wouldn't allow it to deter her from doing her job of taking down the bad guys.

"Do you have evidence to make a case against him?" Michael asked.

Sylvie nodded. "I'm ready with everything I need when the time comes."

"Does he know you have it?"

"I don't think so. Only a couple people do."

Michael asked, "Who?"

"My most trusted team members. Carla and Preston, of course, and…Reggie. But I think Smitty also knows. Reggie must have told him, because Smitty said something today back at the station that leads me to believe so. He made it sound like I'm keeping things off the books. I document every call, but this file is hidden for protective reasons."

Roni shook her head in denial. "I can't believe Shawn would break the law. He's such a sweet guy who everyone adores. He's funny, and whips those Legends cars around the track faster than anyone I've ever seen."

"He races the same type of car Jaxon does?" Ian asked. "They're so small. I can't believe an adult can fit in them."

"Shawn's not a tall man. It's like the cars were made for him, and he was definitely made for racing them. He draws a big crowd and delivers great wins."

"Well, as long as I am chief, he won't win this one," Sylvie stated. "As soon as my probation period is over I'll have more capabilities to make a case without the threat of Dolan firing me."

Michael cleared his throat. "Chief Laurent, like I said, I don't want to overstep, but it appears this Shawn Dolan knows your plans, and will hold nothing back to stop you. Not even the trigger of his gun. I have to ask you, are you prepared to die over this?"

Ian felt her hand stiffen in his. "Not gonna happen," he said to assure her, as well as himself. "Not with me watching her back."

Sylvie tilted her green eyes his way. Appreciation filled them, but he also recognized a stern rejection of his offer.

"Just try to stop me," he dared.

"I have a gun."

"That you've lost once already."

"I will use it if I have to, Ian."

"What's another hole in my body if you're safe?"

"I don't need you."

"Yes, you've made that perfectly clear many times, yet I'm still here. Anything else you want to throw at me? I can go all day."

Sylvie pursed her lips in anger, then quickly gave in with a short laugh, but not before she stuck out her cute little tongue in his direction.

Ian stilled at her bright-eyed smile. Her face lit up the room and for this moment took away the darkness surrounding them.

If only they could stay in this moment.

FOURTEEN

Ian surveyed the station's parking lot for any potential threat. "Wait." He grabbed Sylvie's forearm before she stepped out of the cruiser.

"I've already secured my surroundings. I was scanning the lot before I pulled in. There are three cars. One is Carla's, and the other two were impounded. The tree line is clear. Thanks to bare branches, I can see far into the woods. It's safe." She pushed the door wide and Ian kept up with her brisk gait to the front entrance.

He reached for her hand. "It's not safe, though. How can you go on with work as usual when you know someone wants you dead?"

She looked down at where they were linked, but his hand stayed firm. Let her get used to the feel of him. Maybe she would grow to welcome his touch, want him to reach out more, and not just for help, but for comfort and affection.

She ripped her hand away.

Maybe not.

"I'm a cop, Ian. I make people mad at me every day. Doing my job means stopping criminals and bad people from succeeding in breaking the law. The key words there are *bad people*. I wouldn't expect anything else but retaliation. That's part of being bad. But part of being an officer of the law is serving and protecting my jurisdiction. I go in. Remember? That means I don't run home and hide whenever someone might decide to get back at me for ruining their plans. It also means I put on the uniform and come back here every day."

"With no one to protect you."

"Well, usually that would be Preston, but with him being injured…"

"With him being injured, that leaves me."

"I shouldn't allow it. It's too dangerous, but…but I am grateful you were there for Jaxon when he went to the bridge." She exhaled, proof that she understood the gravity of the situation, the danger still lurking. "I thank God he's safe, but it's time to get back to work." With that she unlocked the door and made her way inside.

She didn't make it five feet before she squeaked to a stop on the linoleum.

"What's wrong?" Ian asked.

"Carla's desk is empty." Sylvie grabbed the butt of the gun at her waist. Her footsteps barely made a sound as she walked around Carla's work space, glancing at the contents on top.

A cola can, tipped over and lying in its own sugary spilled contents. Her cell phone in the mess.

"Carla," Sylvie called, searching through the empty bull pen. "Her car's out front. She should be here."

Ian went to pick up the can.

"Stop." Sylvie's harsh voice halted him. "Until I say otherwise, don't touch anything. Any tampering with the scene contaminates trace evidence."

She walked to her office, the door still closed as she'd left it. With the boarded-up window, visual access inside wasn't possible. On a flash, she pushed the door wide and pointed the weapon as she burst inside.

He ran in to follow. She stood by her sofa where her son had slept just hours ago.

Jaxon was gone.

Sylvie's head lifted and turned slowly to look at Ian. "There's a note." Her lips trembled, her face paled. "He's been taken." She read the typed note to him on a growing cry.

How does it feel to be separated from your family? Come to the bridge or get used to a life without your son.

Sylvie stumbled back. Her knees bent and Ian reached out just in time before she crumpled to the floor.

"I've got you. You hear me, Sylvie? I've got you."

A wail escaped from deep down inside her and she let Ian fold her into his arms. He could feel her gun against his shoulder, and he reached up to take it from her. Her fingers dug deep into his back, as though she struggled to hold on for dear life. "Sylvie, a crime has been committed here. I need you to tell me what to do. What would you do if this was anyone else's child?"

She stilled. Slowly pulling away, he saw the horror in her wide, darkening eyes.

"Stay with me and tell me what I need to do. What we need to do. You said yourself, you can't go home and hide. Stay with me, and tell me what comes first."

At her shaky nod and sniffle, he knew the stoic Sylvie was back to work. She reached to her belt. "All units, this is your chief. Carla and Jaxon are missing. A note left behind points to a kidnapping. I'm issuing an APB for them both. I want checkpoints set up on the edges of town. Stop every car. Do you copy?"

"Smitty and Reggie here. Copy that."

"Buzz and Karl copy."

The rest of her team returned the radio call except for Preston.

"Preston, do you copy?" Sylvie asked. "Preston," she called again.

"The hospital kept Preston overnight," Reggie responded.

"Good to know. I'm also going to need two of you to go to Mayor Dolan's house to notify him."

Silence returned over the radio.

"Do you copy?"

"I'll go," Smitty responded.

"If he's not there, find him. If you can't, I need to know. I'm going to the covered bridge. I'm supposed to go alone, so be discreet when you arrive."

"10-4," her team signed off with their orders.

The map Sylvie had been studying earlier still sprawled across her desk. The tiny letters jumped around the page, making it impossible for Ian to understand. Jaxon's crutch lay on top of it. Ian was sure it hadn't been there before. Had there been a fight between the boy and his kidnapper? Had the crutch been thrown onto the desk?

"He left his crutch. He would need it to walk. Why wouldn't he take it?" Ian asked.

"Another reason I need to get to the bridge. He can't get away on his own."

"I'm going with you."

"You can't. I won't risk Jaxon's life. Or yours. The note says come alone or he dies. This one I have to do by myself."

"But why the bridge?"

Sylvie frowned. "It's where I hid the Dolan evidence. That's why I want Dolan found. If Shawn Dolan is MIA, then perhaps he's Jaxon's kidnapper." With that, she took the gun from Ian's hand and walked out.

He raced to the door. "If not me, take one of your team."

Sylvie pointed to Carla's desk. "They have one of them already. And the rest will meet me there. I hope."

The exit door slammed behind her, leaving Ian alone and feeling useless. A feeling he'd had for far too long. Ian the Idiot came shining through at a moment when he needed to be something else. He needed to be daring and brave, smart and quick. He needed to be like… like his family. He needed to be a Spencer.

But I am a Spencer.

"I am a Spencer," he said in frustration to the empty room. "I am a Spencer," he repeated. The message wasn't meant for anyone but himself—the only person stopping him from taking back what had been stolen from him.

His name.

His home.

His family.

His inheritance.

But he had been wrong about the kind of inheritance. It wasn't money that made him Luke Spencer.

His inheritance was his identity.

It was how God saw him.

The man Jesus was willing to leave His throne for.

The real Luke Spencer behind all the circumstances.

That's who he wanted to be…again.

"I am Luke Spencer. And today I'm taking it all back."

Sylvie said she saw brilliance in him. It was time to dig deep and find that brilliance.

Luke turned to Jaxon's crutch. He nearly reached for it but stopped when he saw the leg pointed to a small outline of a house.

A cabin was drawn on the map.

It had to be a message from Jaxon, one that didn't need to be read with letters.

"What are you trying to tell me, Jaxon? Did you know where you were being taken? God, you've brought me this far. Is this where you're leading me next?"

Luke grabbed the map in one crinkling swoop and headed for the door. He knew the answer was a yes, but first, he had a stop to make.

Every brilliant person has a team, and he was going to claim his.

Sylvie pulled her car up to the desolate campground and parked in front of the covered bridge. The darkened interior displayed only a shadow of a single person too wide to be Jaxon.

Where was her son?

She exited cautiously, her gun at her side, ready to take aim. Her boots crunched in the snow as she made tracks to the mouth of the bridge. The person at the other end came into view.

Sylvie's boots hit the old wood boards with thuds. At the halfway point, she could see enough to make an ID.

Carla.

"Carla, where's my son? What's going on?"

"Where's the file? Just give me the file and this all goes away."

"Goes away? My son's been kidnapped. Someone tried to kill him. Please tell me you're not a part of this.

You were supposed to protect him. How could you do this to me? To Jaxon? You love him. Please rethink what you're doing and stop this before it goes any further. Tell me where Jaxon is. Please."

"I have a gun," her dispatcher said. Her voice shook on the last word.

Sylvie looked to Carla's hands as she stepped up to her, just a few feet away.

"Your hands are empty."

Carla didn't say a word. She only stared at Sylvie, except she wasn't looking at her eyes. Carla latched on something above Sylvie.

"There's a target on me, isn't there?"

Carla swallowed hard. "Where's the file?"

"Someone is forcing your hand. Is it Shawn Dolan?"

"Just give me the file and nobody gets hurt."

"Is that what they told you? I think it's safe to say they lied to you."

"Please, Sylvie. There's a gun on me, too," Carla rushed out with a tremble.

Sylvie holstered her gun and stepped back. She reached the loose floorboard. Jaxon had found the board when he was younger and it became his secret place to hide his trinkets.

She lifted it now.

Nothing lay beneath.

Sylvie bent low to see if the drive had shifted, but even in the growing darkness, she could tell it was gone.

On bended knee, she dropped her head, trying to think of her next move. Things could go really bad from here. She lifted her head to see Carla fidgeting. The woman glanced over her left shoulder. Whoever had taken her and Jaxon was behind her on the mountain somewhere. But how far? At the top, or nearby behind a tree?

"Come on, Sylvie. Hurry!"

"It's not here."

Carla's face drained. "Don't play this game right now."

"I'm not playing a game. I'm serious. The file is gone. I put it under this board—"

A blast from the mountain echoed through the air. Sylvie waited to fall from the gunshot, but found herself flinching involuntarily and not hitting the floor.

She didn't fall, but Carla did.

Sylvie rushed forward and turned her dispatcher and friend over in her arms. She dragged her into the shadows of the bridge. Carla's eyes opened wide, but after a few gasps, her eyes fluttered closed.

"Carla!" Sylvie looked to the mountains as she grabbed her radio. "This is your chief! I—I'm at the covered bridge. Carla's been shot." Blood covered Sylvie's shaking hand.

"On our way, Chief," Reggie responded.

Sylvie watched the mountain. "Did you get Dolan?"

"Wasn't home. His wife says she hasn't heard from him in two days."

So he could be on the mountain taking shots now.

"Tell the paramedics the GSW went through Carla's right lung. She's bleeding out fast."

"Two minutes," Reggie responded. "But your man should be there before that."

My man?

A whiny motor reached her ears from somewhere far off.

A snowmobile.

Sylvie searched the mountains. A single sled and

driver came barreling down the mountain. The red-and-black suit told her it was emergency-personnel attire. It was one of her men.

Is that what Reggie meant?

The sled came screaming up to her and skidded to a stop at the back entrance of the bridge. A face lay hidden behind a black helmet. Sylvie held her breath waiting for the driver to remove the shield and reveal himself.

But instead of lifting the helmet, the driver lifted a gun.

Sylvie drew her weapon.

"Drop the gun and get on!" a male voice bellowed, but with the motor she couldn't ID it.

His gun aimed at her cued her to do as he demanded. He'd already proven he would shoot. With one last look at Carla, Sylvie released her gun to the floor and raised her empty hands.

Plans B and C whirred in her mind as she stepped forward.

As though the man could read her mind, he pushed back and yelled, "Drive!"

Sylvie climbed on and immediately felt the gun push into her back. She still wore her bulletproof vest, but at this close range, a bullet could cause serious damage, even death. She could only hope that man Reggie mentioned would get here soon.

Or was this the man Reggie meant? Perhaps Reggie wasn't sending help, but a killer.

Stalling came to mind, but the gun moved to her head and changed it.

Sylvie zipped the sled back up the mountain, but without the proper gear, the cold temperatures instantly cut through her like a knife. Frigid wind smacked her in the face. Her hands stiffened with instant pain. But none of the dangers she faced from the elements came close to the danger behind her. She may be in the driver's seat, but a killer was now in charge.

FIFTEEN

Luke raced past Sylvie's empty cruiser on his snow-mobile and drove through the covered bridge. A body lying on the other side stopped him on a sliding skid. Carla lay unconscious, blood pooled out behind her. He jumped off and knelt beside the woman, feeling for a pulse.

She was still alive, but barely. He lifted his visor and spoke. The radio inside the helmet he'd taken connected him to backup. "This is Luke Spencer. I'm at the bridge. Carla is still alive, but Sylvie is nowhere to be found. Snowmobile tracks tell me she's been taken up the mountain."

Sirens neared. "We'll be there in a matter of seconds," Buzz replied.

"I hear you, and I'm going up after her."

"Watch your back."

"He won't get me a second time." Luke leaned over the dispatcher. "Carla, help is on the way. Hang in there."

The woman's eyes remained closed as two ambulances screamed up to the bridge's entrance. The paramedics jumped from the vehicles and thudded across with a stretcher and bags.

She would be taken care of from here.

Luke ran back out from the bridge, but before he jumped on the snowmobile, bullets sprayed the snow at his feet. He retreated back.

"Hey, Michael!" he shouted into the radio. "I've got a shooter separating me from the sled. Do you see where they're coming from?"

Luke looked up just as his grandfather's CIA helicopter crested the mountain peak. Gunshots sounded from one of his men standing at the side opening.

"We've got you covered, Luke," Michael spoke through the radio from above. "Go get her."

Luke took a deep breath and raced forward. He didn't let the air out from his lungs until he had the sled zipping away from the bridge and up the trail following the tracks left behind.

The path narrowed and grew steeper. Snowy pine trees smacked him as he raced past them. He wondered how Sylvie had fared coming through here without the right gear. The higher he went, and the lower the sun dropped out of the sky, the more the cold seeped through his gloves and stiffened his fingers. She had to be in agony. Snowflakes began to fall, at first in a light flurry, but quickly changing to a heavy dousing the higher he went.

"Michael, I'm going to need a little direction. I've lost her tracks. Can you lead me to where that cabin is supposed to be?"

"According to the map, you're not that far off, son. Stay to the right. You'll soon come to a stream you'll need to get across."

"Got it. And thanks for being my eyes."

"Anytime."

"Apparently so. You even make holiday hours. Probably not how you planned to spend Christmas."

"Are you kidding? I live for this stuff. What's not to love about a high-speed holiday?"

Luke grinned beneath his helmet. He kept his gaze straight ahead, but felt protected knowing his grandfather hovered overhead reading the map for him. Sylvie would say his resourcefulness was shining through. He never let his dyslexia stop him from gaining the knowledge he needed to learn. So what if his letters danced in wavy lines? He'd found a way to make his path lead straight to Sylvie. And it started with his family.

Sylvie killed the sled's engine and stared at Reggie Porter's mountain log cabin. It stood hidden beneath a canopy of snow-covered pines. Her masked captor pushed his gun into her back. "Move it!" he yelled.

She listened for a familiar voice…like Reggie's.

"Is Jaxon here?" she said, hoping for a reply. With the weight Reggie had lost, the gunman could be him.

No answer came. Just the gun pointed her way.

The whomping sound of a helicopter closed in from somewhere beyond the trees.

Without hesitation Sylvie ran out from under the trees to get the pilot's attention. A bullet from the masked man's gun sent her flailing through the air. She crumpled against the cabin's steps, her lungs emptied in a whoosh. "Who…are…you?" she asked, gripping her chest. Pain radiated in her rib cage. She unclipped the vest to check for the bullet, but a kick to her leg stopped her.

"All you had to do was give Carla the file," the guy yelled. He grabbed her arm and dragged her up the steps, tossing her inside on the wooden floor.

Nausea rolled and her whole body shook. Grabbing at her ribs, she didn't think the bullet had gone through the vest and touched skin, not like in Carla's case. "So you shot Carla?"

"You think I shot her with this?" The guy slammed the door behind him and held up his 9 mm. "I didn't, and believe it or not, I saved your life."

"So you could kill me up here? If you're going to claim to be a hero, then at least show your face."

With that the guy walked past her. He opened a door and a minute later, he reappeared with Jaxon bound and gagged.

"Jaxon!" Sylvie pushed past the pain to kneel. Her son fumbled his way on his boot to meet her before she gained her feet. Sylvie wrapped her arms around him, ignoring the throbbing in her ribs the contact caused. She would rather face the pain than ever let go of her son again. "Are you hurt?"

Jaxon's soft hair pressed against her face as he shook it back and forth. His mumbling voice reminded her of the gag. She pulled the tied cloth down. Immediately, he rushed out a rapid cessation of frantic words. "I heard a gunshot! I thought you were dead. Oh, Mom, I was so scared!"

"Shh, I'm okay. I'll be bruised, but the vest did its job. It's all good, Jaxon. Nothing to worry about."

"So he did shoot you." Jaxon twisted from her grasp. "You promised! You said you wouldn't hurt her. You wouldn't hurt anyone. You lied!"

The man in the helmet stood by the window, looking out to the wilderness beyond the smudged glass.

"She'll live. For now."

"Who are you?" Sylvie asked. "What do you want?"

"I want the file. Give it to me, and I'll disappear from your life forever."

"I don't know where the file is. It wasn't where I hid it on the bridge."

The guy pointed his gun at her again. "I don't believe you. Hand it over, and I'll ride out of here with you both alive and well."

Sylvie couldn't distinguish the muffled voice through the thick helmet. "Are you Shawn Dolan? You're about his height."

"I said give me the file!"

"And I said I don't have it."

"I know where it is," Jaxon said quietly.

"What?" She startled at his confession. "How?" She searched his guilty face. He avoided eye contact and stared at his bent knees.

"That's what I went to the bridge for yesterday. I didn't just go for a walk. I went to get the file. I'm so sorry, but I knew that's what Bret was looking for. He told me you had a file on his dad. He tried to get me to give it to him. He punched me after school one day. He said you were trying to break his family up. He said if you did, then he would do the same to us." Jaxon swallowed. His lips trembled.

"So you went to the bridge to get it? How did you know it was there? You haven't hidden anything in there in years."

He shrugged. "I wanted to use the hiding place again."

"For what?" Sylvie felt the wedge between her and her son double in an instant. It was more than growing distant. He'd also been hiding things from her. "Jaxon, are you doing drugs?"

"No!"

"Then what could you possibly need to hide from me so badly that you would start using your old hiding place?"

"You won't understand."

"Try me," Sylvie said, then thought of a better way. "No, trust me. Come on, Jaxon, it's always been just us. We made a pact, remember? You can trust me."

He nodded. "I know. It's just personal."

"Does this have anything to do with your poems?" She tried to keep her voice calm.

His face jolted. "Yeah. I didn't want you to find them so I went to the bridge a few weeks ago to hide them, but when I lifted the board I found the envelope with the drive in it," he said in one long fast rush. "I put it back, but I thought it might be what Bret was attacking me for."

"What did you do with it?" the masked man demanded, still watching from the window.

"Do not address my son." Sylvie released Jaxon and pushed to her feet, blocking the guy's view of him.

A sick laugh erupted from behind the helmet. Her reflection in the visor shrunk back at the sound.

The next moment the guy lifted the helmet off his head.

Greg stood before them, an angry glare on his face. "Except he's my son, too. And he better start talking or he'll be getting more than a broken-up family. He'll be getting a dead mother."

Sylvie lurched her body at the man who had treated her so cruelly fifteen years ago. How dare he kidnap them and threaten their lives now. Her hands reached out to knock him to the ground. They hit the floor with astounding force and rolled.

Greg threw her off his back, but something inside Sylvie, smothered for so long, must have contributed to a strength she'd never believed possible. She was a mama bear pushed past her limits. Perhaps all these years training to be the best cop she could be had really been preparation for the day Greg would return to hurt her again. Had she always known it would come?

Sylvie elbowed his hold on her arm away, kicking back into his knees at the same time. He bent his head down in pain, and she twisted around to slam his nose back toward the ceiling.

Blood splattered the wood above as well as spraying lightly across her face.

"Ah!" Greg hollered in pain, holding one hand to his face, leaving the other to hold off her assault. "Stop! Just stop!"

He might as well have been speaking a different language.

Sylvie went in for his throat, landing on his chest with her forearm across his neck.

Greg gurgled and twisted with all his strength.

"I will kill you if I have to," she said, inches from his face.

Greg stilled. "Can't…breathe."

"I know."

"Please."

"I'm going to release you, but then you are going to tell me exactly why you are back in town. And spare me the melodrama about it being a desire to have custody of a child you never wanted to begin with. Got it?"

No response.

Sylvie pushed into Greg's trachea a bit more. The pressure sent his legs kicking and body twisting again. His voice strained with incomputable words.

She released the pressure. "I said, got it?"

"Y-yes," he struggled to say, but it was enough for Sylvie to let off her hold enough for him to converse.

Releasing him entirely was out of the question, even

if he'd been disarmed in the takedown. She reached for her cuffs at her back and flipped Greg over with her knee to his back. *Click, click*, and he was apprehended.

She left him facedown to stand guard above him. She reached for his tossed 9 mm on the floor and checked the chamber for the ready bullet. She circled him slow and steady, each footfall creaking on the floor until she came around to his face. The tips of her boots brushed his hair.

Greg lifted his head and dropped it again, unable to hold it up. "You broke my nose."

"'And though she be but little, she is fierce.' That's what Ian says about her," Jaxon informed Greg with a smug smile.

"Who?"

"Jaxon means Luke Spencer," Sylvie said. "You remember him?"

"Oh, your rich boyfriend." Greg spat blood from his snarled lips.

"Boyfriend?" Jaxon asked. "What's he talking about?"

Greg laughed. "Keeping secrets from your son, are you, Sylvie?"

"Nothing, Jaxon. Luke is only a friend. Why don't you go back into that room while Greg explains why he's back in town," Sylvie said. "I'd hate to have you see the ugly tactics of my job. Even though this man isn't a part of your life, I'm sure the things you'd see would pain you almost as much as him." Sylvie stepped on his fingers just enough to show she meant what she said.

"Okay!" Greg shouted.

Good, he heeded her warning.

"I came back to break your little family up. Believe it or not, it would have saved your life."

"Saved my life? You shot me!"

"I shot your vest."

"FYI, you still could have killed me. I could be bleeding internally right now and die before nightfall. You'd go down for killing an officer of the law."

Greg sagged and whimpered. "I just wanted to make him go away. To end his blackmailing once and for all."

Sylvie pursed her lips. "You're back in town because someone's blackmailing you? What did you do wrong that you would commit murder to cover it up?"

"I didn't plan on committing murder. I thought if I separated you from Jaxon that would be enough. I figured it would hurt you more than any life-ending bullet."

Sylvie glanced to her son, who'd yet to move. The thought of losing him did bring on a painful effect that surpassed the bruised ribs ailing her. "Go on."

"But going to court for custody would cripple me, especially with your boyfriend's money. You don't think I remember the Spencers? How someone like you ever captured a Spencer's attention is mind-boggling. Especially with that manly attire."

"You mean my uniform? It's not about fashion. It's about being practical. You never know when you'll have to take someone down. Shall I demonstrate again?"

"No."

"Then keep talking. What did you do that has someone blackmailing you?"

"I've cheated on a few races."

"That's all?"

"They were important races. They boosted my career."

"Ah, and someone found out. Was it Shawn Dolan? I think I remember the two of you being chummy when we were younger. Is he your blackmailer?"

Greg's mouth remained zipped.

"I'll take that as a yes. So he blackmailed you to return to Norcastle to hurt me, either by taking Jaxon from me or by death. Either would work for him. And if you didn't comply, he would report you and have your prize cups stripped. Correct?"

Nothing.

So far she had nothing to arrest Shawn Dolan on. She needed a confession.

"You'll find out soon enough. When I don't deliver that file, he'll be at this door to collect it himself."

"Who will? Tell me who wants that file enough to kill for it! Is it Shawn Dolan?"

"I want a lawyer."

As much as she wanted to scream, Sylvie kept her cool. "You're going to need one, but fine, we'll do this your way." To her son, she said, "Jaxon, where is the file?"

"I'm sorry, Mom."

"You are forgiven. Whatever you did with it, I forgive you. Just tell me where it is."

"I gave it to Bret."

Sylvie pressed her lips tight. "Okay, when?"

"The night I went to the bridge. That's the real reason I went. Bret took his Legends car and drove over to the bridge. I gave it to him."

"Bret was driving the Legends car that night?"

"Yeah, why?"

"I had a little run-in with it on my way to find you. It came out of nowhere and nearly hit me. I followed it for a little while, but without lights, I lost it. Plus, my tire had been blown out. When I pulled over to change it, I was ambushed, knocked out and kidnapped. Preston was also pushed off the road."

"By Bret? I hate him!"

"Stop. We need to keep our heads clear and figure this out. Know who our enemy is and be prepared for when they arrive. Or even better, go get them first."

The sound of a loud motor had her running to the window. The helicopter was back. It was hard to see it with the tree growth all around. She also didn't think the cabin could be seen from above. She wasn't even sure if this was help or more danger coming her way.

"Let's go, Jaxon." Sylvie helped her son to his feet. "Can you walk on your boot to get to the sled?"

"A little. Where are we going?"

"To get the file."

"From Bret?"

"He's apparently kept it from his father, or Greg wouldn't have to bully it out of us. That tells me Bret has had an eye-opening experience with what he found on it."

"But what about...Greg?" Jaxon nodded to the man on the floor. Sylvie took note that he didn't call the pathetic man his father. "Are we just going to leave him here?"

Sylvie grabbed Greg's helmet and handed it to Jaxon. There would be no more hiding for Greg. And by the end of the day, she would be able to say the same for Shawn Dolan. "He won't get far with no gear." Sylvie took his boots off just to be sure. "Don't worry, Greg. You'll be in a nice warm cell by Christmas."

The man grunted but kept his face down on the floor. His life as he knew it was over.

Sylvie helped her son to the door, but when she opened it to the darkening night, a shot echoed through the air, splintering the doorjamb an inch from her head.

Jaxon screamed and fell to the porch. She went down after him.

"Are you hit?" she demanded.

"No," he cried in fear. "I don't think so."

Sylvie squeezed her eyes shut. *Dear God, I'm calling out to You again. You've always been with me, a Father for my son. I'm begging You now to please get him off this mountain safely.*

The helicopter's blades grew louder by the second. Would there be gunfire from above as well as the trees?

Another shot blasted through the night. Sylvie fell over her son to block him from flying bullets. She needed to get the vest on him. With quick work, she ripped it from her shoulders.

"I'm putting the vest on you," she said as she pulled his arms through the openings.

"What about you? What will protect you?"

"Don't worry about me. I'm going to get you out of here. But if something does happen to me, promise me you will keep driving down this mountain. Understand?"

"Mom—"

"Understand?"

Jaxon sniffled. "Yes, I understand."

"God is with you, Jaxon. You won't be alone." At his nod, she said, "Okay, on my count, jump on the front and start the engine. I'll ride on the back. Do you follow?"

"10-4."

She smiled at his use of police code. "When I say go, this will be the fastest race of your life. I know you can do it." She waited for him to take a deep breath and let it out. "Go!"

Sylvie lifted her son with all her strength. Putting

her body in front of his, she twisted around to run backward toward the sled. She tossed him to the front, and was already getting in place behind him when he had the motor up and running. The snowmobile jerked her so hard she nearly fell off the back when Jaxon put it into motion.

Bullets whizzed by her exposed head. She heard them over the motor of the sled and the engine of the helicopter above. A glance up and she saw someone rappelling down the chopper ahead of them.

Jaxon whipped the sled into a spraying side stop.

Sylvie saw the guy land and come running at them at the same time she noticed what had stopped Jaxon from going any farther.

The headlight of a lone sled faced them ten feet away. In the dark, all she could see was a driver in black, a helmet blocking his identity.

"Sylvie!" the guy from the helicopter coming at her from her right called out. She pointed her gun at him and then at the sled rider, and then back at the man coming at her again. In the dark she couldn't be sure who the good guys were. "Sylvie! It's me, Wade. Let me have your son."

"Wade!" she shouted. "Yes, take him. Take him to safety!"

Wade lifted Jaxon off the sled and suddenly rose up off the ground and into the air with her son securely in his hold. She moved her aim to the rider before her. He also took aim with his gun.

"Drop it!" she shouted over the motors. He may not be able to hear her order, but he could read her lips with his light on her. If he said anything to her, she couldn't tell. All she could make out was his shadowed figure and the unmistakable outline of a gun aimed at her. "I said drop it! I will shoot to kill!"

She felt the whiz of the bullet flying past her left ear before she heard the shot. The man had shot at her.

Before she pulled her own trigger, she was jolted from behind. Someone had rear-ended her, sending her forward.

Or had that been the person the shooter had fired at? Perhaps he hadn't been shooting at her, but protecting her from the one sneaking up on her from behind.

But who was the shooter, then?

She brought her sled under control and whipped it back around to see both riders coming at her. Her headlight glowed on an emergency uniform, and she realized it was one of her men.

Reggie's words came back. *Your man is on his way. Your man.*

Was it Ian?

No, not Ian. Sylvie knew beyond a doubt this was none other than Luke Spencer.

The helicopter hovered above, and she knew the Spencers had come to help her. A whole family affair, including the long-lost golden child.

But her man?

Why would Reggie call him that? Luke Spencer wasn't her man.

The rider who had rear-ended her took aim at her. Luke raced his sled at the gunman, slamming into the side of his snowmobile and flying off his own to push the gun away.

The weapon exploded in the night.

Sylvie's heart squeezed so tight, she would have thought the bullet entered her own chest.

In horror, she watched Luke's body jerk back with

the force of a blizzard wind, once again taking a bullet meant for her.

He landed on his back in the deep snow, a billow of the flakes scattered around him. Sylvie had no time to assess the damage done to him and could only hope his bulletproof vest blocked the slug. The shooter took aim at her and pulled the trigger before she could even raise her gun.

When no bullet came her way, she realized his gun had jammed. He banged his palm on the handle and took aim again. The extra second allowed her to get her own shot off.

Her bullet clipped his shoulder and sent him back down in his seat. It also sent his gun flying into the darkness. Sylvie pulled the trigger again, but the driver hit the sled's gas and raced away in time to send her second bullet askew.

Sylvie turned to sit back in her seat and go after him, but a quick glance back showed Luke lying motionless in the same position he'd landed.

A blotch of red grew large in the snow on his right side.

Sylvie jumped off her sled and fumbled her way to him in a cumbersome run. The snow went past her knees. Her body fell and landed a foot from him. Sylvie crawled and fell again, unable to reach him fast enough.

"Luke!" she yelled, her throat clogged with tears. Her bare hands touched his gloved one, and she pushed her body up to land closer to him. With the depth of the snow, she couldn't kneel beside him without sinking. "Luke, can you hear me?"

He made no movement in response. She reached to his helmet and pushed the visor back to reveal an unconscious Luke Spencer.

Snowflakes falling from the sky hit his face and collected peacefully on his lashes.

Sylvie leaned over him to judge where the bullet had gone in. She felt for the edge of his vest and followed it down to his right side. Wetness came away on her fingers when she reached a spot the vest had left uncovered. The bullet had entered under his armpit and blood poured out at a deadly rate. It must have hit the axillary artery. She remembered when Reggie went in for his cardiac surgery, he'd said the doctors were going in through his axillary artery. She didn't need a medical license to know this needed to be clamped or he would bleed out.

But what could she clamp it with up here on a snowy mountain?

She grabbed at her head in frustration, tearing her hair from her ponytail. Her silver hair clip loosened from her head. Sylvie yanked it out and tested its strength. If she could locate the vein she might be able to stanch the blood pouring out of him with it.

Warm blood had her small fingers slipping in their search. When she thought she found the artery she squeezed it and noticed how the blood slowed. "I found it, Luke. I found the vein. Stay with me." And what? Die from exposure up here instead of bleeding out? She wondered what was crueler. All she knew was that neither worked for her. Luke couldn't die. He had a family to claim. She couldn't believe God would keep Luke alive as a baby and bring him back here only to die when he was so close to becoming a Spencer again.

Sylvie's fingers slipped. Another onslaught of blood poured around her hand. She quickly relocated the vein and clamped it again. She grabbed her hair clip and opened it wide enough to cover the sides of the vein and let it close tight. She kept her other hand on the vein and slowly released to test the strength. Blood seeped, but it didn't gush.

And then it broke.

"No! No!" She rushed to find the vein again. But now what? Would letting go be kinder? Could she even let go?

She gazed upon his face, so peaceful. More snow had found its way inside the helmet. She brushed the flakes away gently. She should close the visor from the elements, but doing so felt like giving up. It felt like saying goodbye.

This wasn't how she thought their goodbye would be. She knew it would come, but she was okay with that because he would finally be with his family. She would be able to walk away knowing he was loved.

Now he would die on a mountain because of her.

Sylvie sniffed and felt the tears flow down her cheeks. Slowly, she leaned over him and laid her head on his chest.

"I'm here, Luke. I'm right beside you. You're not alone. I'll be by your side the whole time. I promise."

She reached for the visor to pull it down.

"Luke, are you there?"

The sound of Michael's voice came from inside Luke's helmet.

He had a radio.

Sylvie's heart rate sped up with hope. She rushed forward to speak, but her words tripped over each other. "It's Sylvie. Luke… Help." She took a deep breath and tried again. "Luke needs help. He's been shot and is bleeding out."

"We're on our way back." Michael's words had her shaking with anxiety.

"You're going to make it. Do you hear me, Luke? You're going to make it, even if I have to hold your artery with my hand the whole way." Her fingers pressed tighter. "You're going to make it," she said again to confirm her belief. "You're going to spend Christmas with your family."

The helicopter's motor grew close. Soon it hovered above them and the rope fell off to their side. It jerked with movement as Wade descended a second time. He was by her side reaching for Luke as he landed in the snow.

"I have to hold his artery!" she shouted to be heard.

"I've got him, Sylvie."

Wade's hand covered where she held on and took over.

"Promise me you won't let go!"

"I had to let go once before. That's never happening again!"

She knelt back and relinquished Luke to his family.

"I'll send the rope down for you!"

A team of snowmobiles flew out from over the crest, coming her way.

Her team had arrived.

"No! Get him to the hospital!" she shouted. She would ride down. Besides, she had a couple arrests to make.

She watched as they zipped back up to the helicopter in record time. The chopper flew away as she knelt in the snow, covered in Luke's blood. Fresh snowflakes quickly worked to cover the presence he left behind. The approaching engines reminded her of her sworn duties.

Sylvie stood, climbed on the sled and waved for her men to follow her to the cabin for the first arrest. Greg would get that jail cell tonight. Shawn Dolan would be next.

She knew she'd clipped him. He'd sped off to lick his wounds, but he couldn't hide forever. He had to know the jig was up. But that only made him more dangerous. Sylvie would be keeping a sharp vigil until she had him in custody. She didn't expect him to make it easy. He would go for the kill.

But so would she.

As Sylvie pulled up to the cabin and hauled a defeated Greg out to her men, Reggie stood by her sled, his helmet off. "What happened to Luke?"

"He took a shot meant for me. Again."

"Bad?"

She gave a single solemn nod. "He's with his family now. They'll take good care of him."

Sylvie climbed on her sled, but before she took off, Reggie handed her his helmet. He removed his vest and handed it over to her.

She stared at it hanging there between them.

"Someone wants the chief of police dead. You're our family, and we protect our own."

At her acceptance of his duty, his gloves came next. He stuffed one of her bloody hands inside his glove. When the inside warmth touched her hands, she realized how frozen her appendages were. It was almost like her whole body had somehow distanced itself from her situation.

Reggie lifted her second hand to stuff it into his glove. "I'm going to pray for your man. I'll pray he comes home to you."

Sylvie shook her head. "He'll go home to his family. He's waited long enough."

"Family isn't always about blood. They're the people your heart claims."

"My heart can make no claims on Luke."

"I wasn't talking about yours. I was talking about his." Reggie walked to his sled. Once in his seat, he waited for the chief to give the signal.

But Reggie's words struck her still. She wanted to take solace in the fact that Luke would finally be able to claim a family of his own, but if Reggie was right, then maybe it wasn't Roni and Wade but her and Jaxon. Even after she'd made it clear there was no room for him in her life.

Or was there?

Sylvie pushed the idea away and dropped her visor. She had a pact with her son. She'd made a promise. It would always be just the two of them. There was no room in her life for Luke.

In her heart, well, that would be different.

Sylvie revved her engine and waved her left hand, speaking into the helmet's microphone to the team. "Time to catch us a bad guy. We ride!"

SIXTEEN

I'm here, Luke. I'm right beside you. You're not alone. I'll be by your side the whole time. I promise.

"Sylvie!" Luke jerked awake. A beeping sound somewhere close by sped up to a rapid cadence. A white tiled ceiling came into focus, then a strange woman's face filled his view. Her dark skin and hair didn't trigger a memory.

Not Sylvie.

"Who are you?" he rasped. "Where's Sylvie? She promised she would stay beside me."

"Now, now, your family's here. Everything's going to be fine. I'm your nurse. We've been waiting for you to wake up all night."

"We?"

She moved her round face away and stepped back to reveal the packed room. A few faces registered, a few didn't.

Still, no Sylvie.

"Welcome back, brother."

Luke turned to his left in time to see Roni step up to his bedside. He shrunk back. "Are you going to punch me?"

"Not today."

He squeezed his eyes tight to pull on a memory. Or had it been a dream?

"I was shot. Again."

Luke opened his eyes to find Wade Spencer.

"You," Luke said. "You were there. I saw you."

Roni said, "Wade carried you the whole way to the hospital."

Wade fisted his hands and his dog, Promise, bounded up by his side. She licked his hands and he began to pet her. After a minute, he said, "Your axillary artery under your arm was hit. I arrived on the scene in our grandfather's helicopter. I rappelled down to get you. Chief Laurent had already located the artery and was working to stabilize it." He swallowed hard. "I've, ah, seen my share of main-artery wounds in war. They're not pretty, but don't give me the credit for saving you. Chief deserves it all."

"Where is she? Why isn't she here?" Luke scanned the room, squinting at the unfamiliar faces, wondering if he should know them.

"I'm Ethan Rhodes, Roni's husband," said a blond, wavy-haired man. A set of baby blue eyes contrasted with his serious face.

"The FBI agent," Luke said when it clicked. "I thought you were undercover."

"Made it home for Christmas."

"Christmas. Did I miss it?"

A few laughs went up in the room. "No, you're just in time." Ethan smiled. "Roni's told me all about you. Filled my ear all night long, actually."

Luke looked at his sister and knew it couldn't have been anything good. "About that, um, you should know I have no intention of taking what belongs to them."

Now Ethan looked perplexed. "I'm not following." He glanced his wife's way.

"Oh, I left that part out," Roni explained. "It's nothing. Just a little misunderstanding. You know how we had so many people coming out of the woodwork claiming to be our brother. We had to be sure he was really him before we could give him his inheritance. We hope you can forgive us, Luke."

"Forgive *you*? What have you done with my sister?"

Ethan chuckled, elbowing his wife. "He's got you pegged. It's not too often you hear an apology from Ron—"

Roni sent a warning glare her husband's way.

Ethan cleared his throat. "Never mind. I'm glad I was able to meet you. I'll have to thank our amazing chief of police for coming to your rescue. I've come to rely on her a few times. She's top-notch."

Luke figured there was a story there, but all he cared about was laying eyes on Sylvie. He looked farther into the room and stopped on the sight of a baby.

"I'm Lacey, Wade's wife," the beautiful mother holding the tiny baby said.

"I remember," Luke said. "We met at Clay's." Luke looked to the baby. "He's beautiful. Luke, is it?"

"Kaden Luke, actually." Lacey smiled a brilliant teary smile. "We were going to make his first name Luke, but seeing as the name was so new for you, we didn't want you to have to share it right out of the gate. I hope you don't mind that his middle name is Luke. It would mean so much to us."

He looked to Wade. "But you don't even know me."

"I know all I need to know. You're my brother, and you have come home. That's all that matters."

Luke dropped his gaze to the baby. His brother and

sister could have both moved on to their own families and left him behind, but instead they were here by his side.

Luke moved to reach his forefinger to the child, but pain skyrocketed right down the arm. He inhaled and pulled back until it subsided.

"Now, Mr. Spencer." His nurse was back readjusting his position. "You need to be still for a while. Don't make me get the doctor in here before the gifts are handed out."

Luke looked straight down the bed to where Clay and his wife, Cora, stood arm in arm. "Gifts? What gifts?"

The two separated to show the window ledge had been turned into a mock fireplace hearth, decked out with all the Christmas trimmings. Tinsel and garland and even a wreath hung in the window. But it was the stockings he'd seen at Roni's house that were all hung and waiting to be distributed that clenched his heart.

"You have a stocking, too," Roni announced and ran to the ledge to remove the one in the middle. She carried it back almost reverently. As she neared, Luke noticed the dulled fabric of reds and greens. This wasn't a new stocking.

"It's yours from when you were a baby. Our mother made them. She wasn't a seamstress, but they were made with love. I think they're beautiful."

Luke reached his good arm for the stuffed stocking and brought it close, squinting to read the embroidered letters.

"It says 'Luke.' She embroidered each of our names on them."

"I can't believe you kept it all these years."

"Kept it and displayed it every year," Roni said proudly.

Luke glanced up quickly. "But you thought I was dead."

Roni looked back at Cora and at the woman's nod, she said, "Every Christmas I would help Cora bring up the decorations, and I would always insist on hanging your stocking. Maybe because deep down I knew you were alive. I was too young to have a clear picture of the crash. When I was finally able to speak, Cora tells me I cried for you constantly. I knew someone had taken you. I knew you were out there and needed us." Roni's lips trembled, but she pressed them tight. Her husband wrapped an arm around her shoulders and pulled her in close to him. But Roni kept her eyes on Luke. "Can you forgive us for not coming for you?"

At Luke's silence, she continued, "I know life was so hard for you. I know you suffered tremendously at the hands of your kidnapper. We should have—"

"No. Stop," Luke demanded. "Stop right now. Whatever happened thirty years ago was not our fault, and we cannot blame each other and we can't blame ourselves for it. To do so would mean they won. Maybe you're willing to lose, but I'm not."

Roni's eyes widened. She pulled away from her husband, nearly pushing him over. "Lose? I *never* lose. And don't you forget it."

"I wouldn't dare. You might hurt me."

"That's what big sisters are for. Gotta keep the little brother in line."

The two smiled at each other for the first time since they met.

Family. So this was what it was like. And probably why Sylvie wasn't here. Hospital policy of family only. But the room didn't feel complete without her and Jaxon.

"Thank you for my gift. I thought all I would get for Christmas was two gunshot wounds." He laughed with everyone, but inside felt the pain of another hole, this one burrowing into his heart with each second that went by without knowing why Sylvie wasn't present.

Suddenly, Luke realized someone else besides Sylvie was missing, too.

The man was nowhere to be found. "Where's Michael?" he asked.

Uncomfortable glazes dropped to the floor.

"Wade?" His brother would be honest with him. He didn't know him too well yet, but Luke already knew he was a man who could be trusted.

His brother sighed. "He's, ah, going to bat for Chief Laurent."

"Going to bat for Sylvie?" Luke pushed up. Pain shot through his body, but it meant nothing next to the torture of knowing Sylvie was in trouble. "Was she—she *hurt*? What happened to the shooter?"

"She was fine, but we don't know about the other rider. He took off."

"He's still out there?" Luke pushed up to a full sitting position. The room tilted sideways and nausea rolled up in a wave.

"Whoa!" Ten different hands reached for him before he fell off the bed. It could have been less, but his vision was seeing double, or maybe it was triple.

"Get back in this bed, Mr. Spencer," his nurse said. He wished he could read her name tag, but that was out of the question and it had nothing to do with his dyslexia.

"How am I going to help her? She's in danger." Luke laid his head back on the pillow in torment.

"Michael will do everything he can."

"What happened after I was shot? Tell me everything."

Wade began his briefing again. "The chief got a shot off on the guy's right arm before he took off. Then her and her team came back to town last night, planning the arrest of Shawn Dolan. Apparently, the chief has something on him that has him out for blood."

"He beats his wife," Luke announced to the room. The ladies all inhaled at the same time. "I take it you didn't know. Go on."

"When Sylvie arrived back in town, there was a message from the council, releasing her from her position."

"Why?"

"Well, technically she was still on probation. They don't have to give any reason at all. But with Carla being taken and shot, and the loss of the cruisers and other expensive inventory, they felt she couldn't handle the job."

"Those had nothing to do with her, and everything to do with your town's mayor. Once everyone knows he's behind it all, they'll see she can handle it."

"Except Michael and his CIA team assisted. They're using that as a means to prove she broke the law by working with the CIA on American soil."

"But I would have died, and there was a child. They can't be serious.

"I have to get out of here. I have to help her."

"You're not going anywhere, Mr. Spencer. Over my dead body," his nurse announced.

Luke sized her up. "What's your name?"

"Mary, but some patients have called me Bulldog. I don't take any offense to it. Better make yourself comfortable." Mary leaned back over him as she had when he woke up. "Because like I said, you're not going anywhere."

A knock came on the door.

Luke had to think of a way out of here. Maybe his grandfather could chopper him out by saying he was being transported to another hospital. But using the CIA's helicopter might paint Sylvie in even more of a bad light. It might be best to have Michael go dark with his men.

"Hi, Preston. Any news about your chief?" Wade asked of the person in the doorway. Luke's ears perked up at the mention of Preston's name.

"I'm being released, but I heard Ian was here and I wanted to stop in. It looks like a party in here. I don't want to intrude."

"Forget it, come on in." Wade stepped back to let the officer in. "Glad to see you're on the mend. Any idea who slammed into you?"

Preston stepped into the room, sporting an ugly purple bruise below his eye. He fidgeted with the cuff of his officer's uniform. "Not yet."

"Have you heard about Sylvie?" Luke asked him.

Preston glanced his way with a nod. "I just checked in with the department and heard the news. I'm heading there next. I just can't believe it. Look, Ian—"

"Luke. Call me Luke."

"Luke, I'm really sorry I wasn't there last night for Sylvie."

"You were injured. You wouldn't have been much help."

"But she and I have been together for years, partners long before she become chief. We watch each other's back. I should have been there. I promise, I'm going to stand by her through this. I won't let her down again."

Preston turned to leave.

"Preston, real quick. Can you give her a message for me?" Luke asked.

"Sure."

"Tell her…" He glanced at his family, then at the stockings on the window ledge. There were two more stockings needed before his family would be complete. But knowing her feelings, he would have to get used to it. "Tell her I don't regret anything and I would do it again. All of it."

"I will."

"And thank you for being such a good partner. You mean the world to her." Luke lifted his good arm and offered it to Preston for an olive branch shake. Preston hesitated, then quickly took it. Luke gave the man's hand a firm shake, but when Preston winced, he let go. "Sorry, man, we're both not our typical selves these days. Take care of yourself."

Preston nodded. "I'd say your life is heading into the black. Wish you the best."

The door clicked closed, leaving the room in silence.

"Interesting guy," Cora said with an awkward laugh. "What do you suppose he meant by that?"

"I'll cut him some slack," Clay said. "He's been slammed into and knocked out. You saw his head."

"And apparently his arm. Was he your patient, Mary?"

"When?" The nurse lifted her face from studying a chart.

"He came in yesterday to get checked out after being driven off the road. The hospital kept him for the night."

"Not *this* hospital," she said matter-of-factly. "I've been doing rounds all night. I would have checked in on him."

Luke shot a pointed glance at Wade, who sent one to

Ethan. He didn't have to say a word. His FBI brother-in-law skirted the bed and met Wade by the door in less than a second.

"Wait!" Luke called. "I'm going with you!"

"Oh, no, you're not." Mary shoved him back on the pillow. "Don't make me sedate you."

Luke looked to Roni in near hysteria. He had to get out of here!

A slow smile grew on his sister's face. But it was the wink she sent his way that told him his sister was about to break him out of here.

Luke had to think growing up with her wouldn't have been dull. They might have fought like cats and dogs, but when it counted, she would have been on the front lines to protect her little brother. And if the wheelchair race out of the hospital that preceded a car ride at a speed he'd never thought possible was any clue, life with his big sister would have been a hurricane in motion. Luke was so glad she was on his side…for today anyway. He knew that would change like the weather, but he looked forward to every sibling squabble to come. Being a Spencer never felt so right. Sitting by Roni as they raced into town in her Porsche, he didn't even have to read the Welcome to Norcastle sign to know he was home.

But would he feel the same if Sylvie Laurent wasn't beside him? Or worse, if she could never be because she was killed before he could track her down?

"Can't you go any faster, Roni?"

His sister burst out with a sinister laugh and hit the gas. "You asked for it, little brother. You asked for it."

The weight of her badge always gave Sylvie assurance that what she was doing had value. She placed the metal symbol of authority gently on her desk beside her spare gun, barely making a sound as she did.

Reggie slid them across the desk toward himself and put them in the top desk drawer. "It's only for a little while."

She eyed him dead-on. "You really believe that?"

"No, but what else am I supposed to say? We both know the council is making a big mistake, but neither of us have means to prove it."

"I know it was Shawn Dolan behind everything. If only I still had the file on him to prove to the council he's not the man they believe him to be."

"You know very well you wouldn't be able to release that file without charges being brought by his wife."

"I don't get it. He's hurting her. Why doesn't she want it to stop?"

"Would you want her to just to save your job? Or is it her safety that you care about?"

"Her safety, of course."

"Well, perhaps you could convince her to as a friend now. No longer as chief of police. No one is stopping you from being her friend."

Sylvie smiled for the first time since receiving the notice of termination from the police department that morning. Merry Christmas to her.

"You're right, Reggie. There are many ways I can still help people being hurt at the hands of others." Sylvie reached a hand across the desk. "You're going to make a great chief."

Reggie shook it firmly in both hands. "Not as good as you, and every man in this place knows it. We're losing as much as you are today. More."

"Thank you for saying that. Now, if you'll excuse

me, I'm going to go home and spend Christmas with my son."

"I'd like you to take an escort."

"I'll walk, if you don't mind. There's just something degrading about being dropped off in a cruiser like I did something wrong."

Reggie smiled and came around the desk to walk her out. They made it to Carla's desk. Sylvie touched the empty chair of the dispatcher who had sat in it longer than Sylvie had been alive.

"She deserves a medal. Make sure she gets it."

"Will do, Chief," Smitty said from his desk.

"Just Sylvie," she corrected.

"Always Chief," Smitty responded with nods from her men.

Tears pricked her eyes. A quick blink and an inhale held them in check. "Merry Christmas, team."

She turned away one last time from the men and station and stepped out into the crisp, sunny morning. She passed by her cruiser, which the men had found down by the river. It had been pulled up from the bank and would need an overhaul for Reggie.

She started the short mile-long trek home. Her boots fluffed through loose snow and crunched on the older, harder stuff below. An engine off in the distance had her looking ahead. The red and blue lights sitting on top of the car told her it was a police vehicle.

The car slowed as it approached and the driver's window dropped down as the car came to a stop across the street from her.

"Preston," Sylvie said with a smile. "I guess you heard."

"I'm not happy about this, Sylvie. They had no right."

"They had every right. I was still on probation. You

and I both knew this might happen. You thought it would be from within the department, though."

"That I did, which made me miss the outside enemy approaching. I failed you."

"No." Sylvie crossed the street and approached the car. "Don't ever think that, Preston. You were my right hand, and I'll always be grateful for the years as partners and then your work as my assistant."

He placed a hand over the one she had resting on the car door. He gave it a squeeze and when she thought he would pull the platonic gesture away, he kept it there with a little rub from his warm fingers.

A bit of unease chilled her and she withdrew her hands and stuffed them into her coat pockets. "Well, I better be getting home to Jax. Merry Christmas, Preston. I hope you feel better soon. Sorry you got hurt in all this."

He touched his face but waved his other hand as if to say *no big deal*. "It's all part of the job. And speaking of the job, when I was at the hospital yesterday, I did a little investigating and found out the two hackers who jumped in the river checked in for hypothermia."

The cop in Sylvie stepped to. "Did you get IDs?"

"Of course. You taught me well. They're brothers. James and Brian Miller. A little pressure and they squawked on who hired them."

"Let me guess. Greg Santos."

Preston's face dropped. "Yeah, how'd you know?"

"That was one of the things I got out of Greg before he lawyered up. They're friends of his. He brought them in to wipe out the Spencers' accounts, so Luke wouldn't be able to help me in a custody battle."

"And now? Will the infamous Luke Spencer be helping you?" The edge in Preston's voice brought on another sickly wave of unease. Was Preston angry at Luke?

"What is that supposed to mean?"

"Never mind. Forget I said it. I'm still sore and it's making me cranky. Forgive me?"

She offered a halfhearted smile. "Of course. So, have you arrested the Millers?"

"Not yet. I overheard them talking about meeting someone at the salt tent today. I wanted to come get you to do the honors."

"Me? You know that's impossible now."

"What's the council going to do, fire you? I'll be the one on the books making the arrest. You're just along for the ride. Just like how you took Spencer along for all the rides this past week."

"That's different. I was protecting him from someone who wanted to kill him."

"But no one was trying to kill him. It was you they were after. You shouldn't be out here walking alone on the streets. It's not safe. You better hop in and let me guard you while I go make the arrests." Preston's eyes twinkled with a bit of the mischief she'd seen in them on so many nights working with him.

She smiled back, knowing he was a crucial part of her success in gaining the chief position. He was a true friend.

"I know what you're up to."

"You do?" His eyes darkened.

"Yeah, you always did take a little too much delight in sticking it to the powers that be who feel they can do our jobs better than we can."

"Oh, right. So what do you say? One last ride, Chief?"

Sylvie looked down the road. "Actually, I was going to stop off at the Dolans' and see Andrea. I may not be chief anymore, but that won't stop me from being an advocate against domestic violence in this town. Dolan hasn't seen the last of me, and now he has nothing to hold over me."

"I figured you would do that. Can't let that go, can you?"

"Never."

Preston whistled. "Talk about sticking it. But you know you can't make Andrea Dolan turn her husband in."

"I can at least try to help her see reason."

"But in the end she's going to make the best choice for her life, regardless of what you think she should do."

She stilled at Preston's words. They were her same reasons for her choices through the years. When so many people criticized her every decision along the way, in the end, she made the ones that worked for her.

"You can't fix the world, Sylvie. But you can get a few bad guys off the streets here and there. So what do say? Let's go take these guys and save some innocent people they're targeting with their thefts some heartache. Go out with a bang."

"A bang, you say," she said pensively. "Well, when you put it that way, how can I say no? But we'll have to use your gun. I just turned mine in."

Preston smiled. "I was planning on it."

SEVENTEEN

"She's not at her home and she's not at the department. They also checked Preston's apartment," Luke told Roni as he clicked off her cell. "Wade and Ethan just left her house and made sure Jaxon was safe next door with the neighbor where they brought him last night. But Smitty guarding the place has alerted Jax that something is up with his mom. I was hoping to avoid that. He's been through so much. The kid just wanted to spend Christmas with us."

Roni's sculpted eyebrows raised. "Us? As in Sylvie *and* you?"

"Funny, Sylvie looked the same way when he brought it up. She wasn't thrilled about it, either."

"Don't get me wrong, I'm totally pleased about it. I've been trying to get her to date for years, and now to think she might consider dating my cute little brother, believe me, I'm excited."

"Spending Christmas together isn't a date. She's made it clear that will never happen."

"But you mean to ask her for one as a present, right?" Roni smiled coyly at him.

"First, we need to find her."

She sobered. "Right. Where do you think Preston would take her?"

"I'm trying to think if she mentioned a place that meant something to them, but I don't recall. That worked once for finding Jaxon, but it won't this time."

"Okay, let's think. If all this time it was her partner taking shots at her, where was he taking them from?"

"The first day was at the racetrack. The next time was from the road. I don't see a pattern there. But if he was the one to kidnap her, he would have been the one to bring her to the old mill building." Luke huffed. "He probably left her there unarmed to be killed by those guys when they found her. He wanted them to do his dirty work for him. Sylvie always said that as a cop she goes into the danger, no matter what. Preston probably figured she would barge in on their setup even without a gun, and they would take her out. Preston could mourn the loss of the chief along with the whole town with no worries of ever being arrested."

"Obviously, he forgot the chief is brave but not stupid. So, okay, let's check the mill." Roni floored the gas pedal and they headed downtown to the industrialized section of Norcastle.

It had been days since Luke had been to the apartment he'd rented. Passing by it now he thought of his belongings still strewn about. His Sarno Construction shirt left on the floor, his past as Ian Stone scattered with it. He could honestly never go back to collect his meager belongings, and saw no reason to. Luke instead faced forward and concentrated on putting together his future. Sylvie beside him like she'd promised him on that mountain came into his mind. He couldn't envision his future any other way. He wouldn't settle for a good friend. He wanted more. He wanted her to be his family.

"I think I got it," Roni announced. "Maybe Preston has been in love with Sylvie for years. She's always made it clear she would never date again. But then you came to town. Rich, handsome Luke Spencer turned her head."

"I wish. Anyway, that doesn't jibe. He tried to hurt her and Jaxon before I came to town. He's been planning this all along. I just got in the way." A salt truck rambled by spraying the street. Roni waited for it to pass and pulled up to the old mill building. "There's no sign of them. No car tracks, no foot traffic in the snow. No one's been here since the place was swept." She chewed on her nail as they scanned the area around them. Then she looked back at the departing truck. "I wonder if Preston was the one to rile the townspeople up over the salt tent. There have been picketers for months. If he wanted to hurt Sylvie, he might have created fire where there was only smoke. All the times she kept sending him to calm the crowd, he was probably setting up shop over there and gaining a following."

"So, then he might want her to see his handiwork and take her there."

"I like the way you think. We must be related."

"It doesn't look like anyone's around," Sylvie said as Preston drove up to the tent and pulled around to the back to hide their vehicle. The lot was empty, except for a few plow trucks left in the rear of the parking lot. "The plow drivers are out clearing the streets after last night's storm."

"The Millers are supposed to be here. Let's see if they're hiding out inside."

Sylvie and Preston exited the car and kept in step as they approached the tent on stealthy feet. Preston held his gun at chest level and opened the door first, while Sylvie backed up off to the side. "This is like old times, partner," she whispered. She couldn't think of a better finish to a career than to end it as it began.

"It's not over yet," Preston whispered back. "On my count, you run in. I've got your back…as always." At her nod, he counted, "One, two, three."

"Hands up! Police!" she yelled and ran into the cavernous tent. The stench of salt pricked her nose and watered her eyes, but from what she could see, the place stood empty of any other people. She walked the makeshift aisle between piles of rock salt. There was nothing to hide behind straight back to the rear of the tent, where the salt reached near the ceiling. Some sunlight breached the ceiling fabric and she could see corrosion on the beams.

"I thought you said you had been keeping an eye on this place and the picketers didn't have any cause to make a ruckus." She pointed to the damage. "What do you call that?" She turned just as Preston stuck a rectangular plastic box with a red light blinking in the corner onto the tent interior wall.

Sylvie studied the object, then his emotionless face. "Is that what I think it is?"

"A bomb? Yes. It's a plastic explosive. And there's more than one."

Sylvie's thoughts tripped in confusion. "M-more?"

"They're all over town. The opera house, the town-square clock tower, the covered bridge, even the race-track's grandstand will be coming down momentarily. They're set to go off one after another, and no one will be able to stop them."

A shiver raced up her spine as her body temperature dropped instantly. Chills shook her appendages as an image of the pure chaos that was about to ensue flashed in her mind. She couldn't believe it was Preston who was about to cause such terror and destruction.

"Why are you doing this, Preston?" Her voice sounded desperate to her ears. "Why?"

"To stick it to the town, of course. Just like I said. One last bang. Maybe I should have said 'bangs' as in multiple, because there are so many."

Bile rose up from her stomach. "Just how many? Like more than the places you just mentioned?"

"One more."

A groan escaped her throat. "No, Preston, I don't want this. Please tell me you don't have these positioned where there are people."

"Don't worry."

She sighed in relief.

But then he said, "The hackers will go down for it."

"Meaning people *could* get hurt? Oh, Preston! What are you thinking? The bombs go off, and I'll be the one to take the Millers in? Is that your plan? To get my job back? I'm supposed to be some hero? This is crazy, Preston. Where is the other bomb located? Tell me!" She swallowed hard. Could she hope people wouldn't be out of their homes because of the holiday?

"The Spencer mansion garage, where they house their fancy-schmancy cars." His eyes flashed bright... and deranged. He'd have to be to come up with a plan like this. "It will look like the Millers were going after the Spencers personally again."

All Sylvie could think was the whole family would be there.

Luke.

No, Luke was in the hospital. His family would be with him, but there were still people at the house.

But it was also so far from town. Could she get all the

bombs confiscated in town *and* the one on the Spencers' home? Or would she have to go up the mountain and let the ones in town detonate and hope no one was nearby?

She reached for her phone. She needed Reggie. "Ugh! No connection."

Click, click.

Sylvie raised her gaze to the familiar sound and met the black abyss of the inside barrel of Preston's gun.

No, not Preston's gun...*her* gun. Her missing gun. "Preston, why do you have my gun? The one taken off me when I was dumped at the mill?"

"Drop the phone."

She did as he said and the missing piece to her puzzle slid in. "It was you? I don't believe it. It's been you all along?"

"Yes. Now kick the phone over to me."

Sylvie kicked it across the concrete, her hands raised up behind her head. "You don't plan on me bringing anyone in. You never did."

"Unfortunately, you're not going to make it in the scuffle with the Miller brothers. You'll get a shot off on each of them, but they'll turn the gun on you and kill you."

"And when does this all go down?"

"It already has." He looked at his watch. "Ready? Wait for it. Five, four, three, two, one."

An explosion off somewhere downtown blasted through the serene holiday morning.

Sylvie jerked and covered her mouth at the sound.

"There goes the bridge."

The bridge?

She ran to Preston's left to get to the door, but a quick leg out sent her sailing through the air, colliding with a pile of rock salt. She landed in a slump against it. Granules slid down the pile like a mountain avalanche of displaced snow. As the salt spill slowed, a man's hand protruded from the side of the heap right by her head.

Sylvie fumbled backward at the shock of seeing a human hand pointing at her in its rigor mortis state.

One of the Millers, she could only assume.

"Please, Preston, tell me you didn't do this. Please tell me you didn't kill them."

"Actually, ballistics will show you did."

"Me?"

He waved the gun around. "With your gun. After this place blows, the weapon will be found, along with your body, or what's left of it, and prove you were here to do the deed."

"But why me?"

"Because you couldn't leave well enough alone with Shawn Dolan. The man wanted to put my name out there to lead a special task force with the governor, but if you ruined him, his word would mean nothing. I've tried to bring this up to you. I've proven that I'm worth more than the menial tasks you give me. But every time I brought it up, you shrugged it off. This was going to be my big break, to do something other than cruise around the streets of Norcastle for you for the rest of my life. But you, you just couldn't let Andrea's whimpering go. You had to keep building a case against Shawn, trying to convince his wife to tarnish his good name. If only I could find the file you created on him. I searched your house and Evergreen. Anywhere I could think you hid it."

"Wait. That was *you* who broke into Evergreen? *And* my house to leave the message? You broke procedure about the safe house and put Mrs. Clemson at risk just so you could look for the file?"

"That's not all I broke. I even broke my nose to give me some time away from the station to look for it."

"And to get rid of me. Don't forget that."

"I couldn't. Shawn made it very clear that I couldn't. Get the file and make this case go away, or there would be no governor's job for me. But I knew even if I found the file, you were never going to stop. You said so yourself this morning. Dolan thought if you lost Jaxon, it would break you and take your searchlight off him while you fought a custody battle. He dragged your useless ex back here to take Jaxon from you, but I knew that wouldn't be enough. I knew the only way to stop you was to silence you forever. If Spencer hadn't shown up and ruined everything, I would be celebrating with Mayor Dolan right now and all would be well."

"*Well?* What about Andrea? It's physical abuse."

"Andrea didn't want your help. Nobody wants your help."

"Well, they're going to get it anyway. Tell me how much time until the other bombs go off."

"Why? So you can save the town? You don't have what it takes."

"How much time?" she shouted.

As she'd hoped, Preston checked his watch. "The clock tower blows in five min—"

Sylvie took the brief moment given to her and threw herself into the air at him. Her focus was his right arm, which held the gun. With her right shoulder she landed and jammed it into his chest, shoving him back while her right hand grabbed the gun and pushed out to his side. It would be harder for him to take aim again if she moved the weapon away from his body. At the same time her left hand banged into his wrist so hard it cracked.

Preston screamed out in pain. "My arm! You broke my arm!" His lips snarled as grunts and growls were directed at her.

Sylvie responded with the gun now turned on him. One press of her finger and it went off.

Preston went flying back to the cement floor. His head slammed hard, knocking him out cold. Blood pooled out behind him as she approached him. The shot went through his left shoulder.

"I don't have what it takes? Take that." Her rapid breaths pushed against her ribs. "Now you have a hole to match the other one I gave you last night." She leaned over Preston and felt for a pulse. "You'll live to stand trial, though. Then you can tell everyone about your… aspirations."

The door swung open. Luke stood on the threshold. "Sylvie!" He rushed in. "I thought…" He looked at Preston on the ground. "I thought that was you. Are you all right?"

"Get out!" she yelled, halting him. "Now! There's a bomb!"

Sylvie reached for Preston's dead weight and attempted to drag him out of the building.

Luke moved in beside her.

"Didn't you hear me? I said get out!"

"I'm beside you, Sylvie. I won't ever tell you not to do your job, but I will stand beside you while you do it."

She searched his face, breathless at the words she thought she misheard, but prayed she hadn't. "Do you mean that?"

"Only if you promise to never let go again."

"I thought…"

"I know what you thought. That what I needed was my family. But that includes you and Jaxon, too."

She slowly smiled, then nodded on a cry. "Help me get this maniac out of here, so I can kiss you."

"Gladly."

It dawned on Sylvie that Luke was injured and should be in the hospital, but as they dragged Preston's body far away from the shed, it felt so right to have him beside her.

Her man.

They dropped Preston in a snow pile, and none too gently.

Luke reached for her, but she held a hand up, remembering the other bombs. "No, wait. You need to get your family out of their house." She grabbed Preston's radio off his shoulder. She pushed the button. "This is Ch— This is Sylvie Laurent calling for Reggie."

"What's your location, Sylvie?" Reggie called back. "I'm sending the chopper to pick you up."

"Salt shed. You need to get a couple of bomb squads together. Five is more like it. There are plastic bombs set to go off all over town."

"Bombs?" Luke said. "Where are they located? And why does my family have to leave their house?"

Sylvie looked at Luke while she told Reggie the locations. "The salt shed, the opera house, the bridge, the clock tower, and…"

Luke raised his eyebrows waiting for her to tell him.

Sylvie felt her lips tremble. "I'm sorry, Luke." To Reggie she spoke loud and clear. "The Spencer mansion. It's in their garage."

Luke's face paled as Roni walked over to them from her Porsche. "My family's there by now." He spoke as though he hadn't fully comprehended the weight of it all yet.

Luke said, "We'll never make it in time." He grabbed

the radio from Sylvie. "Reggie, this is Luke. I need you to contact Michael Ackerman. He needs to get to my family's home and get everyone out."

The radio answered with static, then Michael's voice came over. "Already on it, son. I have Reggie in the helicopter with me. I just told Wade. He and Ethan are taking care of it as we speak. The question is, does the chief want my men's help in diffusing the rest of the bombs in town?"

Luke glanced her way, his eyebrows raised. Sylvie shook her head and said, "That call's up to Reggie now."

Michael chuckled. "Actually, you're chief again. Reggie is awaiting your command."

"What? How?"

"The council changed their minds when they read your file. They realized their illustrious mayor had a reason for wanting you gone. He's been arrested."

"Arrested? But that means…"

"It sure does. Andrea Dolan and her son are pressing charges. Bret gave them the USB with all the evidence you'd collected. But we'll get to that later. Right now I need direction from the chief of police. Do you want my men's help?"

"Yes!"

Michael laughed again. "Good, because they're already on the ground. And I'm on my way to pick you up."

"Preston's been shot and he's unconscious. I'll need to go with the ambulance."

"My helicopter will be faster. I don't want that guy dying."

Before Michael clicked off, she said, "Michael, I need to know—were there any casualties in the explosion?"

"We're looking into it, but we're thinking everyone

was home for Christmas, where they belonged. You did lose your bridge. You'll be needing a good builder. Have I told you how handy my grandson is? Brilliant, really. I've seen his work."

"Your grandson?" Sylvie looked at Luke and said, "He says you're brilliant. You want the job?"

"What I want is you in my arms, now."

Sylvie looked to Luke's arms outstretched to her, open and...*bleeding*?

"Luke! You popped your stitches." She rushed for him.

"I know. It's just a couple, though. I felt them pop, but I'm okay."

"Are you sure? You could start bleeding out again."

"Well, to be on the safe side, I'll have Mary the Bull-dog take a look at them when we get to the hospital."

"Who?"

"Oh, wait until you meet her. I think you'll like her. She's got the same commanding voice you do."

Luke flashed a grin her way, and she made her way into his arms.

Luke pulled her in closer with his good arm and threaded his fingers through her hair. With a gentle tug, he pulled her head back to lift her face to his. His ice-blue eyes danced with a happiness that had to match her own.

Luke let out a huge sigh. "Hey, Roni," he called to his sister. "I think I'm finally home."

Roni let out loud whoop that made them both laugh before growing serious.

"Home," Sylvie whispered a breath away from him and closed her eyes. "Now about that kiss."

Luke took her lips in his typical no-holds fashion. Fast, sure and with abandon. Everything that she saw in

Luke Spencer, and she loved it. She loved his kisses. She loved his presence that didn't suppress her, but made her stronger. She loved him, and as she let herself love him, her arms reached around his neck and gave his exuberance right back to him. She was never letting go again.

And neither was he. She knew it without a doubt.

The helicopter blasted over the trees and came down in a snow-stirring landing, but the two of them were oblivious to anyone and anything but them. When someone tapped her on the shoulder, they still held on to each other, but slowly, with a smile on each of their giddy faces they unlocked their lips and looked to the person who had so rudely interrupted.

Jaxon stood less than a foot from them, his eyes wide with…what?

Confusion?

Disappointment?

Anger?

Sylvie's smile slipped from her face. With the sound of the helicopter, she couldn't give her son a very detailed excuse. She opened her mouth and closed it with useless attempts to explain.

But still her arms stayed fastened around Luke. She was never letting go again. But how could she make her son understand?

"Jaxon!" She reached a hand out to him. "I love him, Jaxon. I love Luke! Please understand!"

Jaxon's eyes widened and he looked to Luke.

Luke touched Sylvie's face and turned her cheek to face him, his eyes misting up at her words. She could see he was astounded.

She nodded and mouthed, "I love you."

His lips trembled as a huge smile broke his tanned face. He shouted over the helicopter, "I love you, Chief

Sylvie!" Then he looked to Jaxon and shouted, "I love your mom, and I love you!"

Jaxon reached out with both hands, but before she knew what he planned, he launched his arms around them both. Wet tears hit her cheek, and she knew he was crying with them.

Sylvie felt Luke's sigh of relief. She beamed a smile up at him, knowing exactly how he felt. Without a word, they wrapped their arms around her son and brought him into the fold.

A family they would be. Forever linked and never letting go.

EPILOGUE

The rushing spring water gushed below Norcastle's covered bridge and lifted a cool breeze to the people inside.

Sylvie stood with Jaxon on one side and Luke on her other. Six months had passed and Luke had worked diligently on rebuilding the bridge into a perfect replica of its former rustic feel.

In the crowds around them, too numerous to count, there were many who'd joined in to repair the structure, getting to know the missing Spencer child and coming to love the man he'd become. Almost as much as she loved him.

His old boss, Alex Sarno, had flown in and was here somewhere. He'd come to help, but was pleasantly surprised Luke had it covered. Well, not really surprised. He said he'd always known Luke had a natural talent for building, but something else Alex said really hit home. He said his greatest accomplishment will always be the bridge he'd built, but not this one, as magnificent as it was. It was the bridge he'd built to his family. Alex said he would miss Luke, but wished him well on his own construction business, which he would be full owner of here in the Northeast. Especially because they wouldn't be competing for jobs. He said that with a wink.

Sylvie looked up at her soon-to-be husband and smiled. She dropped her head on his shoulder and he wrapped an arm around her to pull her in close.

"You ready to be sworn in as chief of police, love?"

"Let's make it official…but first, we need to become a family."

A few happy cheers rose up behind Luke. Sylvie peered over his shoulder to see his whole family there with huge smiles on their faces. She returned their grins and couldn't wait to be a part of their clan. Their numbers astounded her, and from the news Roni shared last week, they would be growing again. Sylvie glanced at her friend with her husband's arms draped around her from behind. Ethan's hands rested on Roni's abdomen so casually, but Sylvie knew of his awe for the child growing inside her.

Sylvie moved her attention to Lacey. She made a beautiful mother to her little boy, but right now little Kaden was being loved by his grandparents up from South Carolina. Sylvie wondered if Luke knew his family extended far beyond Norcastle.

Promise barked, bringing everyone's attention to her sweet smiling face. She barked again and ran up to Sylvie to be pet.

"She must sense your jitters," Luke leaned over and whispered to her.

"Nonsense. I've never been surer of anything in my life."

Luke flashed his striking grin, his teeth still so white against his tanned skin. She had to wonder when his tan would fade to match the pale skin of the Northerners, not that she would complain if it didn't. His golden-brown skin just reminded her of how special he was.

"You ready, golden boy?" She smiled.

"I was ready months ago."

"I know. I just wanted to be married on the bridge, and I wanted to be sworn in as chief under my married name, which means I had to wait until the probation period and trials were over."

"The council would have lifted the probation period, you know."

"And take a special privilege? Not my style."

"And speaking of style, have I told you how beautiful you are?"

"Only about twenty times since I arrived, but go ahead, you can say it again. I'm made of sturdy stuff. I can take it."

"No worries about all the flattery weakening you?"

"Funny about that. I think it actually makes me stronger."

Luke leaned in. "In that case, let me compare you to—"

"Stop right there, mister. No reciting someone else's work. Not on my wedding day."

Luke looked past her to Jaxon and winked. "Well, now that you mention it, Jax and I have been working on a little special something. What do you say, Jax? Shall we share it?"

Jaxon gave an emphatic nod.

"You're on, Pastor," Luke said.

The elderly man cleared his throat and began. "Dearly beloved, we are gathered here today to join two people who adore each other and wish to join their hearts as one, along with their families. Luke Spencer and Sylvie Laurent, it is a joy to officiate your marriage to one another. I do believe you have your own vows?"

"Luke's going to wow us with his words," Sylvie said loud enough for all to hear.

She giggled just for him. Then he reached into his tux pocket and pulled out a piece of folded-up paper. Ever so slowly, he unfolded it and any mirth left his eyes. When he focused so thoroughly on the paper, Sylvie's smile evaporated even faster. "Oh, Luke," she whispered. "You're going to read it?"

He gave her a timid smile. "Jaxon and Roni have been helping me. It's amazing how much you can learn when you take name-calling out of the mix. And these have helped, too." He reached into his pocket and pulled out a pair of rose-colored glasses.

"Glasses to help with dyslexia?" She laughed with anticipation. "I always knew you were resourceful. You know what you want, and you go after it."

He locked his eyes on her. "I know a prize when I see one. Not even bullets will deter me from claiming it." He held the glasses up with one hand and lifted the paper. "Now will you let me read? And just so you know, this is only the first of many readings. I have a whole new world to explore with these things."

She beamed at his excitement at finally being able to read. He had a lifetime to make up for. "Well, then, what are you waiting for, Mr. Spencer? Put those lenses on, and let's get this show on the road."

* * * * *

If you enjoyed HIGH SPEED HOLIDAY,
don't miss Wade's and Roni's stories
in the ROADS TO DANGER *series:*

SILENT NIGHT PURSUIT
BLINDSIDED

Available now from Love Inspired!

Find more great reads at www.LoveInspired.com.

Dear Reader,

Welcome back to Norcastle, New Hampshire, for the final story involving the Spencer family and the Roads to Danger series. I do hope you enjoyed meeting Luke, and I just know the Spencer family will grow and flourish in years to come.

I had a wonderful time researching this series by spending time at the racetrack and meeting some great racing families. I really had no idea it was a family affair. I firmly believe families need something to do together, and I would love to know what you do with yours to bring you all together.

As the themes in *High Speed Holiday* exemplified, family and home were what both Luke and Sylvie needed to find their peace, and to find each other. I've enjoyed every minute of writing about them and hope their faith struggles have lifted you up and encouraged you in your walk with God.

Thank you for reading *High Speed Holiday*. I love hearing from readers. You can visit my website, katyleebooks.com. You can also write to me at Katy Lee Books, PO Box 486, Enfield, CT 06083.

Katy Lee

COMING NEXT MONTH FROM
Love Inspired® Suspense

Available December 6, 2016

ROOKIE K-9 UNIT CHRISTMAS
Rookie K-9 Unit • by Lenora Worth and Valerie Hansen
When danger strikes at Christmastime, two K-9 police officers meet their perfect matches in these exciting, brand-new novellas.

CLASSIFIED CHRISTMAS MISSION
Wrangler's Corner • by Lynette Eason
On the run to protect her late best friend's child, who may have witnessed his mother's murder, former spy Amber Starke returns to her hometown. But with the killer on her heels, she'll have to trust local deputy Lance Goode to help them survive.

CHRISTMAS CONSPIRACY
First Responders • by Susan Sleeman
When Rachael Long unmasks a would-be kidnapper after he breaks into her day care and tries to abduct a baby, she becomes his new target. But with first response squad commander Jake Marsh guarding her, she just might evade the killer's grasp.

STALKING SEASON
Smoky Mountain Secrets • by Sandra Robbins
Cheyenne Cassidy believes the stalker who killed her parents is dead—until he follows her into the Smoky Mountains and shatters her hopes of beginning a new life. Now Cheyenne must rely on Deputy Sheriff Luke Conrad to keep her safe from an obsessed murderer.

HAZARDOUS HOLIDAY
Men of Valor • by Liz Johnson
In order to help his cousin's struggling widow and her seriously ill son, navy SEAL Zach McCloud marries Kristi Tanner. And when he returns home from a mission to find that someone wants them dead, he'll do anything to save his temporary family.

MISTLETOE REUNION THREAT
Rangers Under Fire • by Virginia Vaughan
After assistant district attorney Ashlynn Morris's son goes missing, she turns to former army ranger Garrett Lewis—her ex-fiancé and the father of her child—for help finding him. But can Garrett keep Ashlynn alive long enough to rescue the son he never knew he had?

———————

LOOK FOR THESE AND OTHER LOVE INSPIRED BOOKS WHEREVER BOOKS ARE SOLD, INCLUDING MOST BOOKSTORES, SUPERMARKETS, DISCOUNT STORES AND DRUGSTORES.

LISCNM1116